Saadat Hasan Manto, a proud Kashmiri, was the most widely read and the most controversial short-story writer in Urdu. He was born on 11 May 1912 at Samrala in Punjab's Ludhiana district to a family of barristers. In a literary, journalistic, radio-scripting and film-writing career spread over more than two decades, he produced twenty-two collections of short stories, one novel, five collections of radio plays, three collections of essays, two collections of personal sketches and many scripts for films. He was tried for obscenity half a dozen times, thrice before and thrice after Independence. Some of Manto's greatest work was produced in the last seven years of his life, a time of great financial and emotional hardship for him. He died several months short of his forty-third birthday, in January 1955, in Lahore.

Saba Mahmood Bashir is a poet, author and translator. She is the author of *Memory Past* (2006), *I Swallowed the Moon: The Poetry of Gulzar* (2013) and *Gulzar's Aandhi: Insights into the Film* (2019).

WOMEN *of* PREY

{SHIKARI AURATEIN}

- stories -

SAADAT HASAN

MANTO

translated by SABA MAHMOOD BASHIR

SPEAKING
TIGER

SPEAKING TIGER BOOKS LLP
125 A, Ground Floor, Shahpur Jat, Near Asiad Village
New Delhi 110049

First published in paperback by Speaking Tiger Books 2019

ISBN: 978-93-89231-32-8
eISBN: 978-93-89231-33-5

10 9 8 7 6 5 4 3 2

Typeset in Garamond Premier Pro by SÜRYA, New Delhi
Printed at...

Translator's dedication

For Amir and Sana

Contents

Introduction

Saadat Hasan Manto (1912–1955) has always been an enigma. For those who have read him a lot, and even for those who have read only a couple of his stories, or just heard about his colourful personality. Even after the 2015 film *Manto*, directed by Sarmad Khoosat, and the acclaimed television drama *Main Manto* in Pakistan, followed by the biopic by Nandita Das in India, the mystique around the author persists. And as often happens with legends, Manto has also been stereotyped in the popular imagination—in his case, pigeonholed as a troubled genius; a rebel with the terrible gift of 'madness' who only wrote dark and disturbing stories.

Manto's name has come to be synonymous with his short stories set around the Partition, like 'Toba Tek Singh', 'Kaali Shalwar', 'Boo' and 'Khol Do'. Unfortunately, these few stories have eclipsed the complexity, range and versatility of his work. Manto's case is similar, to an extent, to that of his contemporary Ismat Chughtai, who is identified more with her 'controversial' story 'Lihaaf' than any of her other masterpieces. Readers have rarely appreciated the complete oeuvres of these two masters of Urdu literature.

I too did not know much about the vast body of Manto's work, apart from the well-known Partition stories which I first read in translation. I only came across his 'Sketches' about a decade back, which led me to his writings in various other genres. The 'Sketches' were profiles of Ismat Chughtai, Noor Jehan, Nargis, Ashok Kumar and other famous literary and film personalities. In these pieces, Manto was characteristically blunt, even brutal. He wrote what he saw, without mincing any words. Next I read his 'Afsanche' or micro-fiction, as it is called today, with its subtle humour and power, and my journey with Manto got more interesting.

Women of Prey comprises mainly stories that were first brought together in 1955 in a collection titled *Shikari Auratein*. These stories and sketches show a completely different side of Manto—raunchy, mercilessly funny and gloriously pulpy, even when they end in tragedy. These are women trying to pick up men on the streets, women asserting their desire, and men being men and, almost always, fools or hypocrites; enterprising alcoholics, honest thieves, and tragic, talented hustlers. For those who know Manto only for his heart-wrenching Partition stories, this book shows a different genre of writing, presenting him as an accomplished writer of pulp fiction and comedies of manners, as well as a caustic columnist.

Most of the stories in the original manuscript are dated around 1950 and are set in Lahore, Amritsar and Bombay. The themes are entirely 'Mantoesque', but the treatment is rather different from what many readers have been trained to expect from him.

The first story in the present volume is 'Flowers of Divine Mercy', which is about a man who, unable to get his daily drink in peace, comes up with an ingenious plan to drink at home—without his wife knowing. A similar tug-of-war relationship of a couple is on show in 'Haircut' ('Hajamat' in Urdu; its clever sexual innuendo near impossible to capture in English). Both these stories largely progress through simple, but crackling dialogue between the characters. 'Womankind' is about the shenanigans that ensue when a pornographic film is brought to India in the

1940s, and it comes into the life of an unsuspecting married couple.

Manto has often been criticized for writing 'smutty' stories, and stories about sex workers where he makes no attempt at morality, or even political correctness. His argument was that sex, including transactional sex, is an integral part of society and there is no reason why it should be banished from literature. The title story in this book is a series of vignettes, or anecdotes, where Manto or a Manto-like protagonist describes encounters with different women cruising the streets of Lahore and Bombay for men. They are fearless and audacious. Nowhere does Manto mention that these women were prostitutes. He portrays them as independent, single women, alone at night or in the day, taking lifts from men they do not know. In fact, the only story where prostitution is hinted at features a man.

There are two profiles in this collection, 'Meerut's Sharp Wit' and 'Sitara', both of actors from the Bombay film industry. 'Meerut's Sharp Wit' was published in the original *Shikari Auratein*, while 'Sitara' has been added to this volume as it gels so perfectly with the the other pieces in this collection that showcases Manto's talent for the dramatic, the sensational and the irreverent. 'Sitara' is an incredibly indiscreet yet strangely admiring portrayal of an incredible, admirable woman—the legendary Kathak dancer Sitara Devi—and her insatiable appetite for men. Translating these two pieces was an enriching experience in another way. It led me deeper into the life and times of Manto—and all his friends and acquaintances—in an unusual manner. For instance, Paro Devi's profile, 'Meerut's Sharp Wit', led me to other literature on the film industry of the 1940s and '50s. After translating the story of this genteel courtesan and aspiring actress from Meerut, I read more about all the film personalities who appear as the supporting cast—Ashok Kumar, Gyan Mukherji, Wali Saheb, Mumtaz Shanti, Rai Bahadur—and the dynamics between all of them. I read about how films were actually written and made in those days, and the kinds of problems faced by the industry in pre-Independence India. The sketch on Sitara Devi led me to stories about Nazir, K. Asif, P.N. Arora, Mehboob and the making of *Mughal-e-Azam*, among other fascinating material. I watched a number of Sitara's dance videos on YouTube, trying to decipher that compelling figure—an astonishingly free-spirited woman, far ahead of her time. From the people, my focus soon shifted to the different studios of the time—Bombay Talkies, Film City, Ranjit Film Studio, Cinetone among others—that brought us classics such as *Kismet*, *Anarkali* and *Nagin*. They were places that Manto came to know well.

In some of his sketches and stories, Manto also takes us through the lanes and by-lanes of Bombay—through Bhindi Bazaar, Mohammad Ali Road, Clare Road, Lady Jamshedji Road to Khudadad Circle and Hall Road—bringing alive the world of Bombay cinema of the 1940s, with its all its glitz, glamour, parties, heartbreak and scandals.

These stories are not just about 'hunters', but also about the 'hunted', the unfortunate and the downtrodden. The story titled 'Gentlemen's Brush' revolves around a beautiful man—always dressed in a spotless black achkan—who goes around dusting rich men's coats, getting close to them. But the service leaves him deprived in an unexpected way. 'Three and a Half Annas' is another sobering story, about the absurdity of imprisoning the hungry and the poor for petty theft, and the sheer immorality of the law.

~

Manto's descriptions of the characters and the cities they moved through are so vivid that it actually takes the reader back in time. Whatever one reads from his pen, it is clear that Manto was a man of his times. Be they his early days in India or his latter days in Pakistan, his writings always reflected the socio-political upheavals, the hypocrisies, the madness and the bleak comedy of his era.

What we know about Manto is largely from his autobiographical writings. He was born in Ludhiana, Punjab in 1912 to a family of barristers with Kashmiri ancestry. His early education happened in Amritsar. Manto was around seven years old at the time of the Jallianwala Bagh massacre. He witnessed the protests and demonstrations that erupted afterwards, which must surely have a mark on his young mind. Perhaps, they sowed the first seeds for his bleak worldview, and his sensitivity to injustice.

As a student, Manto was not among the brightest. Strangely, he failed twice in Urdu in high school. After barely clearing the exam in the third attempt, he joined the Hindu Sabha College in Amritsar. Here too, he failed the year-end exam twice, and eventually dropped out. His poor performance in Urdu may have been because his mother tongue was Punjabi. But all the same, it was in Urdu that he excelled later in life.

It was around this time that Manto tried his hand

at translating European classics into Urdu. Starting with Victor Hugo's works, he went on to translate Oscar Wilde and books by Russian masters like Maxim Gorky. In *Another Lonely Voice: The Life and Works of Saadat Hasan Manto*, Leslie Flemming quotes Krishan Chander about the early influence of Russian literature on Manto.*

Leaving Amritsar to attempt another stint at university, Manto came to study at the Aligarh Muslim University. But this time he had to leave soon afterwards, because of his ill-health. He stayed at Batote in Kashmir for a few months to regain his strength and then returned to Amritsar. He then left for Lahore to work at the newspaper *Paras*, but he didn't stay there for long, either. Finally in 1936, he left for Bombay to edit the weekly film magazine *Musavvir*, and it was from this point that his life took a turn. He published his first collection of short stories, *Atish Pare*, that year, which had not only political but romantic stories as well.**

Three years later, Manto married Safiya. Although he remained in Bombay till the Partition of the

---

*Leslie A. Flemming, *Another Lonely Voice: The Life and Works of Saadat Hasan Manto* (Lahore: Vanguard Books, 1985), 36.

**Ibid., 38.

country, they came to Delhi in 1941-42, with Manto working for All India Radio and writing radio plays. He published over four collections of plays in his lifetime—*Aao*, *Manto ke Drame*, *Janaze* and *Teen Auratein*. Flemming maintains that these eighteen months were actually Manto's 'golden period'—apart from the radio plays, he published short stories, including the controversial collection *Dhuan*, along with his first collection of topical essays, *Manto ke Mazamin*, during this time.*

Despite this 'golden period' in Delhi, scholars argue that it was his stay in Bombay that shaped his writing and gave him his distinctive style. In their introduction to *The Armchair Revolutionary and Other Sketches*, Ali Mir and Saadia Toor mention that in order to supplement his salary as journalist, he also started working as a junior editor at the Imperial Film Company, and in the course of time, he was writing dialogues and scripts for Saroj Movietone, Hindustan Cinetone, Famous Pictures and Filmistan.** In Bombay, Manto was not only exposed

---

*Ibid., 13.

**Saadat Hasan Manto, *The Armchair Revolutionary and Other Sketches*, trans. Khalid Hasan, ed. Ali Mir and Sadia Toor (New Delhi: Leftword Books, 2016), 11.

to a cosmopolitan culture and people from different walks of life, he also found great friends in the film industry, like Shyam, Savak Vacha and Ashok Kumar. Along with writing for films, he regularly contributed columns and profiles (often controversial) to papers and magazines—profiles of film personalities such as Ashok Kumar, Mehboob, Shyam, and of course Sitara and Paro Devi.

His sensibilities and worldview evolved visibly in Bombay, and he went on to write powerfully and with great insight and honesty about those sections of society which people were unwilling to see or discuss. In etching out his memorable characters and stories, Manto went beyond the glitter and glamour of Bombay, to illuminate the unseen corners, the invisible people of the city. He wrote about sex workers and pimps, beggars and hustlers. He called a spade a spade.

Manto's portrayal of women is sometimes debated. There are different views. But what is undeniable is that he did not always portray women as victims. There are several stories, like some included in this volume, where the women are smart, clever, confident, vindictive and conniving too. There are others where he seems to objectify them. Jerry Pinto, in his introduction to *Stars from Another Sky*, notes how it is 'difficult to tell where Manto stood on the issue of women. The male gaze is deployed time and again, sometimes slyly, sometimes directly.'* But then Pinto draws our attention to the end of the piece on Sitara Devi: 'She [Sitara] is no mere woman, according to the evidence Manto adduces, but a maneater. In three paragraphs, three men claim that their fall from grace, their loss of health, their state of being alone and palely loitering, has to do with the danseuse. And then Manto closes: "In my book, she walks tall. I do not know what she thinks of me but I have always thought of her as a woman who is born once in a hundred years."'**

~

In Bombay, Manto also became a member of the Progressive Writers' Association, which had Leftist leanings. But in the course of time, due to his forthright style and the subjects he chose to write about, he was denounced by his fellow writers. In the

*Jerry Pinto, introduction to *Stars from Another Sky*, trans. Khalid Hasan (Delhi: Penguin Randomhouse India, 2010), xv.

**Ibid., xvi.

essay 'Lord Shiva or The Prince of Pornographers: Ideology, Aesthetics and Architectonics of Manto', Harish Narang mentions that when the story 'Boo' was published in the annual number of *Adab-e-Lateef* in 1944, *Prabhat*—the daily published in Lahore—observed that such stories 'corrupt' the minds of young boys and girls, and 'pollute' the public taste.*

Manto brushed all this aside, though it could not have been easy, for he was sensitive to criticism. Being forsaken by the very people he saw as fellow artists and comrades did take a toll. However, what finally pushed him over the edge were the horrors of Partition and the treatment that he received from the government of Pakistan during the obscenity trials he faced there (Manto had followed his family to Lahore in 1948). Devender Issar in the essay, 'Manto: The Image of the Soul in the Mirror of Eros', has quoted Manto, revealing his desires, aspirations and disillusionments:

> You know me as a short-story writer and the courts know me as an obscene writer. The government

---

*Harish Narang, 'Lord Shiva or The Prince of Pornographers: Ideology, Aesthetics and Architectonics of Manto' in *Life and Works of Saadat Hasan Manto*, ed. Alok Bhalla (Shimla: Indian Institute of Advanced Study, 1997), 69.

> sometimes call me a communist, and sometimes a great literary figure of the country. Sometimes the doors of livelihood are closed on me and sometimes they are opened on me. Sometimes I am declared a *persona non grata* and considered an 'outsider'; sometimes when powers-that-be are pleased, I am told that I can be an 'insider'. I am still troubled, as I have often been in the past, over questions like: *Who am I? What is my status?* What is my role in this country which is regarded as the largest Islamic state?
>
> You may call my concerns fictional, but for me the bitter reality is that in my country, which is called Pakistan and is very dear to me, *I have yet to find a place*. That is why my *soul is restless*. That is why I am sometimes in a *lunatic asylum* and sometimes in a *hospital*. I have still not found *my rightful place* in Pakistan. Nevertheless, I know that I am a significant person. My name is of great importance to Urdu literature. If I didn't have that illusion, my life would have been absolutely unbearable.*

Manto was never at ease in Pakistan. It seemed that his heart was still in Bombay. In his translator's note in

*Devender Issar, 'Manto: The Image of the Soul in the Mirror of Eros' in *Life and Works of Saadat Hasan Manto*, ed. Alok Bhalla (Shimla: Indian Institute of Advanced Study, 1997), 184.

Mottled Dawn: Fifty Sketches and Stories of Partition, Khalid Hasan says that Manto was extremely disturbed when he learnt that Ashok Kumar was receiving hate mail accusing him of inducting Muslims into Bombay Talkies. When the religious tensions were mounting during the time of Independence (his wife and children had moved to Pakistan when it was still a part of India), it was difficult for him to decide which of the two countries was his homeland.*

The countless obscenity trials in Pakistan (he had been dragged to court in pre-Partition India too) took a huge toll on him, getting him blacklisted and increasing his economic hardship. Always a heavy drinker, he became an alcoholic. He was also admitted to a mental asylum. He was a wreck in his final days, and died of cirrhosis of the liver in 1955.

~

One may accept that there is not one, but many Mantos that shine through his writings. Whether he wrote stories that were hard-hitting and forthright, or raunchy and hilarious, he is one of the few writers in Urdu literature whose characters almost always came

*Khalid Hasan, translator's note in *Mottled Dawn: Fifty Sketches and Stories of Partition* (Delhi: Penguin, 2011), xvi.

from the margins. Sharp, intense, ruthlessly honest and fiercely opinionated, Manto was nevertheless, without doubt, a humanist. He was convinced of his genius, and sometimes this made him seem egotistical; and yet, when we read his letters and diary entries, he wasn't always entirely so.

Manto died in January 1955, at the age of forty-two. He had written his epitaph much earlier:

> *Yahaan Saadat Hasan Manto dafan hai.*
> *Uske seene mein fann-e-afsana nigari ke saare israar-o-ramooz dafan hain.*
> *Woh ab bhi manon mitti ke neeche soch raha hai ke woh bada afasana nigar hai ya Khuda!*
>
> Here lies Saadat Hasan Manto.
> With him, lies buried the art of fiction writing.
> Buried under the earth, he is still wondering: who is a greater writer—him or God!

But even in death his words were not heeded, and this epitaph was not put on his grave. It eventually said:

> *Yahan Manto dafan hai jo ab bhi yeh samjhta hai ke uska naam loh-e-jahan pe harf-e-muqarrar nahin tha!*
>
> Here lies Manto, who still believes that he was not the final word in this world!

The travesty continued. The Bombay which still breathes through his writings—where he wrote for the film industry and about the colourful people in it—did not even acknowledge his death. Not a single newspaper or magazine, out of the many that he wrote for, reported on his passing. It is said that only a Pune-based newspaper carried the news in a little corner, that too with his name misspelt as 'Minto'.

Looking at the full oeuvre of his writings, whatever the genre, it is easy to conclude that Manto was a luminary of Urdu literature, and he was immensely versatile. He defied social tradition, always poking holes in middle-class morality. While this collection introduces readers to newer, unforgettable characters, the most enigmatic character of all is still Manto. With every story, yet one more attribute of his personality comes forth, one more shade of empathy, another note of skepticism. If the stories and sketches in this collection are witty and gloriously outrageous, they are acidic and immensely sad too. There are, indeed, many Mantos.

Saba Mahmood Bashir
October 2019

Flowers of Divine Mercy

When the newspaper *Zamindar* showered praise, like the flowers of Divine Mercy, on Doctor Rathar, Ghulam Rasool's friends began to call him Doctor Rathar. Wonder why, as the two men were not related in any way. Doubtless, Ghulam Rasool had failed the MBBS thrice. Even so, there was really no comparison between Rathar and Rasool.

Doctor Rathar was a doctor because of his advertisements which peddled medicines to enhance the male libido. He would swear upon the name of God and His Prophet in describing the miraculous powers of his medicines, and earn thousands of rupees. Ghulam Rasool did not sell such medicines nor did he have any interest in them. He was happily married and did not require anything to increase his sexual prowess. Yet, his friends continued to call him

Doctor Rathar and somehow, he too accepted this title bestowed upon him. Perhaps, because he really had no other option. On the one hand, his friends liked this name and on the other, 'Doctor Rathar' obviously sounded more modern than 'Ghulam Rasool'.

And so, Ghulam Rasool would be addressed as Doctor Rathar. After all, the word of the masses is the decree of God.

Doctor Rathar had innumerable virtues. His greatest virtue was that he was not a doctor and had no desire to become one. He was an obedient son studying in a medical college to fulfill the dreams of his parents. He had been studying for so long that even the building of the college was now an essential piece of his life. He had begun to think of the college as the house of a revered elder, where it was his duty to show up every day to pay his respects.

His parents were adamant that he pass medicine; his father was convinced that he possessed the qualities of a successful doctor. About his elder son, Maulvi Sabahuddin had predicted to his wife that he would become a barrister. Hence, when he was sent to London after finishing his LLB, he returned only after he had become one. Now it's another matter that his practice was far less successful than that of other barristers.

Although Doctor Rathar had failed thrice in the MBBS, his father still believed that he would eventually become a great doctor. And Doctor Rathar was such a dutiful son, that he too believed he would sit in London's Harley Street one day and the world would sing his praises.

Another virtue of Doctor Rathar was that he was a simpleton. But his biggest drawback was that he would drink a lot and he would drink by himself. Initially, he tried hard not to take anyone else along, but his friends started pestering him. They got to know his hideout. They would reach Siwai Bar at seven in the evening, and unwillingly, Rathar would have to pay for all the drinks. These people would talk highly of him, and in his drunken euphoria, Doctor Rathar would empty his pockets for them.

Five–six months passed in this manner. Doctor Rathar used to get 200 rupees as pocket money from his father. He lived separately from his parents and the house rent was twenty rupees. Those were the good days. Still, his wife had trouble managing the household expenses because Doctor Rathar had to pay for his friends' drinks.

Alcohol was cheap in those days. One bottle cost eight rupees; Rathar would take a loan of four and a half rupees. But the situation was getting out of hand as he was taking a loan every day, to buy drinks for his friends. So he thought he would drink at home. But how was that possible! If he drank at home his wife would instantly divorce him. She hated alcoholics. Not only did she hate them, she was also terrified of them. She would get scared seeing anyone with red eyes. 'Oh, Doctor Saab, that man! His eyes were so frightening...I think he was drunk.'

And Doctor Rathar would think to himself: What were that man's eyes like? Do eyes really turn red after drinking? In which case, hadn't his wife seen any red in his eyes? For how long would his secret remain a secret? Surely his mouth stank. How was it that she had never smelt him? Then he would think, 'Maybe because I've always been careful...I turn my face away when I talk to her. Once when she asked why my eyes were red, I'd said to her that some dust had got into them. Another time she had questioned me about the foul smell, and I had brushed it aside saying, "I smoked a cigar, the damn thing stinks."'

Doctor Rathar was used to drinking by himself; he didn't need company. When in his senses, he was a miser too. Besides, his pocket did not allow him to keep paying for his friends' drinks. He thought long and hard about finding a way out of this fix, some way for him to have his cake and eat it too. In other words, a solution that would allow him to drink at home, where his friends would dare not join him.

Doctor Rathar wasn't a full-fledged doctor but he surely knew a few things. He knew that medicines were poured in a bottle and given to patients with the usual message written on them: 'Shake the bottle before use'. With this knowledge, he came up with a plan. He would drink in the house. He would have the best of both worlds. He would pour alcohol in the bottle of medicine and keep it in the house. He would tell his wife that he has a headache and that his supervisor, Syed Ramzan Ali Shah, has prescribed this medicine himself, and has asked him to have it with water in the evening at intervals of fifteen minutes. Inshallah, he would be right as rain.

Doctor Rathar was pleased with himself for having thought up this scheme. For once in his life, he felt that he had discovered a new America. Hence, the next morning he told his wife, 'Naseema, I have a splitting headache. It feels like my head will burst.'

Naseema replied with great concern, 'Then, don't go to the college today.'

Doctor Rathar smiled, 'My dear, all the more reason I must go. I will consult Doctor Syed Ramzan Ali Shah. He has the healing touch.'

'Yes, yes, you must go. Do take his opinion about my problem too.'

Naseema suffered from leucorrhea, which did not interest Doctor Rathar in the least. But he added, 'Yes, yes, I'll speak with him about it. But I am pretty sure that he will prescribe an extremely bitter and stinking medicine for me.'

'Well, you are a doctor yourself. You should know medicines aren't sweet.'

'That is alright, but I hate medicines that smell foul.'

'At least see what medicines he gives you. Why are you thinking like this already?'

'Okay.' Massaging his temples with his fingers, Doctor Rathar left for college. In the evening, he returned with whisky in a bottle of medicine and said to his wife, 'Didn't I tell you that Doctor Syed

Ramzan Ali Shah would prescribe such a medicine? One that would be extremely bitter and would stink? Here, smell it.'

Removing the cork of the bottle, he held it near his wife's nose. She sniffed, and instantly recoiled.

'What a wretched smell!'

'How can I have such a medicine?'

'No, no, you will have to have it. How else will you get rid of that headache?'

'It will go away on its own.'

'How will it go away on its own? This is such a bad habit of yours. You get the medicine and do not take it.'

'What kind of a medicine is this? Looks like it is some kind of alcohol.'

'But you know that English medicines have alcohol in them.'

'Such medicines be damned.'

Seeing the marks on the bottle, Doctor Rathar's wife exclaimed, 'Such big doses!'

Doctor Rathar made a face. 'That's the problem.'

'Now don't call it a problem. Take Allah's name and have the medicine. How much water should I add to it?'

Taking the bottle from his wife's hand, Doctor Rathar said with a pained face, 'Will have to order soda. It is a strange medicine: instead of water, it requires soda.'

To this Naseema responded, 'The doctor must have prescribed soda because there must be something wrong with your liver.'

'Only God knows what all is wrong.'

With this, Doctor Rathar poured a dose into his glass.

'By God, I will *not* have this!'

His wife lovingly put a hand on his shoulder and coaxed him, 'No, no, you must have it. Don't smell it, just gulp it down. That's how I would have my fever mixture.'

With a great tantrum, Doctor Rathar had his first drink of the evening. His wife thumped his back in encouragement and said, 'Another dose in fifteen minutes and by the grace of God, the headache will be gone in seconds.'

Doctor Rathar had enacted the entire charade with such sincerity that he didn't quite feel he'd drunk whisky. But when the headiness actually hit him, he laughed happily to himself. This was a great scheme. Exactly after fifteen minutes, his wife poured another dose, added soda to it and brought the glass to Doctor Rathar.

'Here, have this. It doesn't actually smell so bad.'

Doctor Rathar held the glass and winced, 'You'd know how bad if you had to drink this. By God, it smells of alcohol. Here, smell it.'

'You are being stubborn just like me.'

'Naseema, I swear upon myself, I am not being stubborn. There is no question of being stubborn. But let it be. It's alright.'

Saying this, Doctor Rathar drank up his second peg of the evening.

He finished three doses. He felt a little better but the headache returned the next day. He told his wife, 'Doctor Syed Ramzan Ali Shah has told me that the ailment will take its time to go away, and I must continue to have the medicine regularly. God only knows what name he gave me for this illness. He'd said that, "Had it been an ordinary headache, just two doses would have cured you. But your case is a little serious."'

Hearing this, Naseema said anxiously, 'Now you must have the medicine very regularly.'

'I don't know if I can... If you give it to me on time, I'll somehow force myself to drink it.'

Naseema mixed a dose with soda and gave it to him. When the stench hit her all of a sudden, she felt nauseous but didn't show it on her face, lest her husband refuse to have it.

Doctor Rathar had his three doses after much insistence from his wife. She, in turn, was very happy that her husband was obeying her, because he was notorious for not paying her any heed.

Many days passed. The routine of drinking and being made to drink continued. Doctor Rathar was happy that his ploy had worked. Now he needn't be afraid of his friends. Every evening of his was spent at home. He would have a dose and lie in bed, reading a magazine. Exactly after fifteen minutes, his wife would come with the next dose. Then, even without asking for it, he would get his third drink. Doctor Rathar was very satisfied. Many days had passed, and this process of drinking had become a comfortable routine for him and his wife.

One evening Doctor Rathar brought a full bottle. He'd removed the label and told his wife, 'The chemist is a friend of mine. He told me, "You have three doses every day and it is turning out to be expensive for you. Take the full bottle. Pour some every day into the smaller bottle with markings and have your three doses. It will turn out to be very reasonable for you."'

Naseema was quite pleased to hear this. This would help her save money. Doctor Rathar was also happy, as he too had been paying more, buying three drinks a day. He could buy the entire bottle for eight rupees.

One day, when Doctor Rathar returned from college, he found his wife in bed. He called out to her, 'Naseema, serve the food. I'm very hungry.'

Naseema responded in a strange manner, 'Food? Haven't you already eaten?'

'No, I haven't!'

Naseema drawled, 'Noooo...you have already eaten. I had given it to you.'

Doctor Rathar was startled. 'When did you give me food? I've just got back from college.'

Naseema yawned and said, 'Don't lie...you didn't go to college today.'

Doctor Rathar smiled, assuming that Naseema was joking. 'Come, get up now. Serve the food, I am starving.'

'Nooooo,' Naseema said again, 'You are lying! We ate together.'

'When? This is the limit! Come on, don't be funny. Get up.'

Doctor Rathar tried to pull her up by the arm. 'I swear to God, I am so hungry there's an army of mice on a rampage in my stomach.'

Naseema giggled. 'Mice? Then why don't you eat those mice?'

Doctor Rathar asked in astonishment, 'What has happened to you?'

Naseema assumed a serious air and, putting a hand to her forehead, addressed her husband, 'I...I...I had a severe headache...had...had...two doses of your medicine...the mice...the mice are troubling me... please get tablets to kill those mice...food...I will just serve the food...'

All that Doctor Rathar could say to his wife was, 'Go back to sleep. I have already eaten.'

Naseema giggled loudly, 'So, I didn't lie, did I!'

When Doctor Rathar went to the other room and opened the day's issue of *Zamindar*, he saw the headline, 'Flowers of Divine Mercy Rain upon Doctor Rathar'. The news under it said that the doctor had been arrested by the police for deceit and trickery.

Ghulam Rasool aka 'Doctor Rathar' felt that Divine Mercy had been showered on him too.

Womankind

Ashok met Maharaja G at the race course. And they became great friends after that.

For Maharaja G, owning racehorses was not just a hobby but an obsession. His massive stables had horses of the finest breeds. Just as his palace, the domes of which could be clearly seen from the race course, housed artefacts of all kinds.

When Ashok visited the palace for the first time, Maharaja G spent hours showing him the various antiques, which he had collected from all corners the world. Ashok was highly impressed by the young Maharaja G's taste.

One day Ashok visited the Maharaja to ask about betting tips for the horses, but he was watching a film in the dark room. He invited Ashok right in there. It was a 16 mm film which the Maharaja himself had shot with his camera. When the projector started, the last race was speeding off the screen. Maharaja's horse had won that race.

On Ashok's request, the Maharaja played a few other films. Switzerland, Paris, New York, Honolulu, the Kashmir valley. Ashok was delighted to see all these in colour.

Ashok himself had a 16 mm camera and a projector. But he did not have the treasure of so many films. He had never found the time to watch such films.

After showing a few films, the Maharaja switched on the light and slapped Ashok on his thigh. 'So, tell me, how goes it?'

Lighting a cigarette, Ashok said, 'This was fun.'

'Do you want to see more?'

'No, no...'

'No, you must watch this one. You will enjoy it.' Maharaja G opened a small box, pulled out a reel and mounted it on the projector.

'Watch it patiently.'

'What do you mean?'

The Maharaja switched off the light.

'I mean, watch everything very carefully.'

He turned on the projector.

A white light shimmered on the screen for a few moments, and then suddenly, pictures appeared: a naked woman lying on a sofa; another combing her hair at the dressing table.

Ashok watched in silence. After a while a strange sound escaped his gullet. Laughing, the Maharaja asked, 'What happened?'

Ashok's voice was quivering, 'Stop this, yaar...stop it.'

'Stop what?'

Ashok got up to leave but the Maharaja made him sit back down saying, 'You will have to watch the complete film.'

The film continued to run. There was a wild dance of nakedness on the screen. Men and women in sexual abandon. Throughout the film, Ashok remained uncomfortable. When the film was over and the same white light came on again, Ashok felt that whatever he had seen was his own imagination, rather than the projector.

Switching on the light, Maharaja G looked over at Ashok and roared in laughter.

'What has happened to you?'

Ashok seemed to have shrunk in his seat. His eyes

were squeezed shut because of the sudden light in the room. Sweat glistened on his forehead. Maharaja G thumped him on the thigh and laughed so hard that tears rolled down his eyes. Ashok got up from the sofa. Wiping his forehead with a handkerchief, he replied, 'Nothing, yaar.'

'Nothing? Didn't you enjoy it?'

Ashok's throat was dry. 'Where did you get this... this film from?'

Stretching out on the sofa, Maharaja replied, 'From Paris...Pahree...Pahree.'

Ashok shook his head. 'I don't understand...'

'What?'

'These people...I mean...how can these people...in front of the camera...'

'That is what is amazing, isn't it?'

'It is...' Ashok wiped his eyes with his handkerchief. 'It's as if all the pictures are stuck to my eyes.'

Maharaja G got up. 'I showed this film to some ladies on one occasion.'

'To women?' Ashok shrieked.

'Yes, yes. Women...and they enjoyed it immensely.'

'That can't be true.'

The Maharaja replied with great seriousness. 'It's

true, I tell you. After watching it once, they wanted to watch it again. They would close their eyes, scream and giggle.'

Ashok shook his head. 'This is the limit...I thought they would have fainted.'

'That's what *I* had thought. But they had a lot of fun.'

'Were they European?'

'No, they were from our very own country. In fact, they borrowed the film and the projector from me many times after that...I don't know how many of their friends they've shown it to.'

'I say—' Ashok stopped mid-sentence.

'What?'

'Can you lend me the film for a couple of days?'

'Of course, you can take it,' the Maharaja jabbed him in the ribs. 'Whom will you show it to?'

'To friends.'

'Go and show it to anyone you want,' said Maharaja G taking the reel out of the projector. Putting it in its box, he handed it to Ashok.

'Here. Enjoy!'

A shiver ran down Ashok's spine as he held the box. He forgot all about the horses. And after making small talk for a minute or two, he left.

Ashok screened the film for many of his friends. This nakedness of humanity was a new thing for them. Ashok noted the reactions of every one. Some were slightly disturbed but scrutinized each scene minutely. Others closed their eyes after watching a bit. Some, in spite of keeping their eyes open, could not quite watch the film. One could not tolerate it at all and left midway.

After a couple of days, Ashok thought of returning the film. But then he thought about showing the film to his wife, and took the projector home. At night he called out to his wife. Closing the door, he set up the projector, took out the reel and put it on. Switching off the light, he played the film.

A white light shimmered on the screen for a few moments, and then the pictures appeared. Ashok's wife screamed out loud. Trembled. Jumped. She let out a strange sound. Ashok tried to pull her back but covering her eyes, she started screaming again.

'Turn this off! Turn this off!'

Ashok laughed, 'Arre, watch it... Why are you shy?'

'No, no,' she tried to break free and run away.

Ashok tried to pry away the hand that covered her eyes and pulled her to himself. But she began to cry.

Ashok stopped, a little bewildered. It was only for pleasure that he had shown her the film.

Crying and muttering, his wife opened the door and left the room. For some time Ashok sat staring blankly at the naked pictures flashing in front of him, the images which were indulging in beastly acts. It was then that he understood the delicacy of the situation. The realization pushed him to the depths of humiliation. He thought that he had committed an extremely shameful act. He was embarrassed that this realization had not come to him earlier... He'd shown it to his friends, that was alright. But to do that at home, show it to his wife...his own wife? He broke out in a sweat.

The film was still running. Naked women were still writhing and dancing on the wall. Ashok got up and turned off the projector. His head and heart were drowned in shame. He wondered how he would ever face his wife again.

The room was pitch dark. Lighting a cigarette, he tried to get rid of the sense of humiliation by trying to think of other things. But he failed. For a while, he again tried desperately to purge his mind of what he had seen and done. But when nothing worked, a strange desire rose in his heart—that there be darkness in his mind, as there was in the room.

He then thought, what if my mother-in-law hears of what happened? What if my sisters-in-law get to know? What will they think of me? That I turned out to be a man of such depraved morals, a man of such vulgarity, that I would subject my own wife to...

Tormented, he lit another cigarette. The pictures of naked women that he had seen so many times, began to dance in front of his eyes again. And behind them he saw his wife's face, stunned by this unimaginable heap of filth. He shook his head sharply and began pacing up and down the room. Even this did not end his restlessness. After a while, very quietly, he stepped out and peeped into the adjacent room. His wife was lying on the bed, with a sheet pulled over herself. He stood there for a long time, wondering what words he could use to ask her forgiveness. But he could not muster the courage. He came back to his room and lay on the sofa. He lay awake for a very long time. And finally fell asleep.

When he woke up in the morning, the incident of the previous night was fresh in his mind. Ashok did not think it appropriate to meet his wife and left for work without breakfast.

In the office he was unable to focus on work. He couldn't rid himself of the feeling of shame and dread. 'Such a vulgar act...and I didn't even realize...'

He tried to call his wife many times. But each time, after dialling half the numbers, he would put the receiver down. In the afternoon, he asked the servant who brought his lunch from home, 'Has memsaab eaten?'

'No, she isn't home. She has gone out.'

'Where?'

'That I don't know, saheb.'

'How long has it been?'

'She left around eleven.'

Ashok's heart began to pound. He was no longer hungry. He ate a few morsels, and then gave up. His mind was in a whirl. Eleven...why hasn't she returned yet? Where could she have gone...to her mother's place? Will she tell her mother everything? Of course, she would! A daughter can tell her mother anything... Or maybe, she has gone to her sisters. What will they say? They used to respect me so much... How far will the news travel? Such a vulgar act and I didn't even realize...

Ashok left the office, got in his car and drove

aimlessly around the city. He couldn't think of what to do. In the end he turned the car towards his house. 'To hell with it! We'll see what happens...'

But as he got closer his pulse started racing. And when the lift rose with a jerk his heart leapt into his mouth.

The lift stopped at the third floor. He deliberated for a while, and then finally swung the door open. As he approached his flat, his feet stopped. He thought of turning back. But just then, the door opened and his servant stepped out to smoke a beedi. Seeing Ashok, he hid the beedi in the cup of his hand and salaamed him. Ashok had no choice but to enter.

The servant followed him in. 'Where is memsaab?' Ashok turned and asked.

'Inside...in her room,' he replied.

'Who else is there?'

'Her sisters, saheb...and the memsaab of the Colaba saheb...and those party women...'

Hearing this, Ashok strode towards the room. The door was shut. He pushed. Then he heard his wife's thin but loud voice, 'Who is it?'

'Saheb,' the servant replied.

Commotion broke out inside the room. Ashok

could hear screams; sounds of doors being unbolted, *khut-khut, phut-phut*. Taking the corridor, Ashok entered the room through the back door and saw that the projector was on. And on the screen, in the clear light of day, blurred human forms were engrossed in a beastly, mechanical dance of lust.

Ashok began to laugh uncontrollably.

Three and a Half Annas

'Why did I murder? How I ended up with blood on my hands is a long story. Unless I explain to you the exact circumstances, you won't understand. And till I do, your conversations will only be about crime and punishment. There are men and there are jails... Because I've lived in a jail myself, my opinion can't be wrong. I completely agree with Manto saheb—prison cannot reform a criminal. But then, this truth has been repeated so many times that emphasizing it makes it a tired party joke, that's been told a thousand times. And it isn't a joke that even though we all know this reality, thousands of jails still exist. Handcuffs, shackles...I have known these bondages of the law.'

Rizvi looked at me and smiled. His thick, black lips quivered strangely. His small, intoxicated eyes glinted like the eyes of a murderer. We had all been startled when he had suddenly joined our conversation. He had been sitting in a chair close to us, drinking coffee with cream. When he introduced himself, all the details of his crime and trial came back to us. We recalled that by turning approver, he had cleverly saved himself and his friends from the gallows.

And now here he was. He had been released from prison that very day. He addressed me in a very polite manner. 'Excuse me, Manto saheb...I'm interested in the conversation that you all are having. I am no writer, but I can certainly say something on this subject in my broken language.' Then he added, 'My name is Siddique Rizvi. I was linked to the murder that happened in Linda Bazaar.'

I hadn't followed the stories about that murder closely. But when Rizvi introduced himself, all the newspaper headlines came to mind.

The subject of our conversation when Rizvi intervened was whether jail can reform a criminal. Even I had been feeling that we were chewing on a piece of stale bread. So I was relieved when Rizvi said that this reality has been stated far too often, and highlighting it any more is like repeating a tired joke. He had spoken exactly what was on my mind.

Finishing his creamy coffee, Rizvi looked intently with his tiny eyes, and asked with great seriousness, 'Manto saheb, why does a man commit a crime... what is a crime...what is punishment—I have given this a great deal of thought. I think that behind every crime, there is a history—a large part of one's life experiences, which can be either good, or twisted. I don't have a degree in psychology, but I know this much for sure—a man does not commit a crime by himself; it happens due to circumstance.'

'You are absolutely right,' Naseer said.

Ordering another coffee, Rizvi said to Naseer, 'I don't know, janab...whatever I have said is based on my personal experience. Otherwise this subject is an ancient one. I think it was Victor Hugo...the famous French novelist...or maybe he was from another country, I'm sure you would know, he wrote a lot about crime and punishment... I remember a few sentences from one of his books.' At this point he turned to me. 'Manto saheb, it was your translation, wasn't it? What was it? "Remove the ladder that takes a man towards crime and misfortune." But then I would think, which ladder is it? How many rungs does it have?

'Whatever be the case, at least this much is certain: this ladder definitely exists, its rungs exist. And as far as I can tell, they are numerous. To count them, to number them, is the greatest of feats. Manto saheb, governments track opinions, governments compile figures, governments document all kinds of things. Why don't they count the rungs of that ladder? Isn't that too their duty? I killed...but how many rungs of this ladder did I climb to become a killer? The government granted me immunity and made me an approver...it did this because it did not have evidence. But now the question is: whom do I ask for forgiveness for my sin? The circumstances that led me to kill are now distant, a whole year separates me from them. Should I then cite this distance and ask for forgiveness or those circumstances, which stand there and mock me?'

All of us were listening to Rizvi very intently. He did not appear to be formally educated but from his conversation, it was obvious that he was well read and articulate. I might have said something to him, but I wanted him to keep speaking and me to keep listening. So, I did not interrupt him.

A fresh cup of coffee arrived. Taking a few sips,

he continued, 'God knows what rubbish I've been talking...but there's one man I've never been able to forget...a bhangi who was in jail with us. He was sentenced to a year for stealing three and a half annas.'

Naseer was surprised. 'For stealing just three and a half annas?'

'Yes, sir...only for three and a half annas,' Rizvi replied icily. 'And even that much was not in his fate, because he was caught. The amount is safe in the government treasury while Phaggu bhangi is not. Maybe because he can be caught again. Maybe because his hunger may drive him to steal again. Maybe because the people who make him clean their piss and shit may not be able pay him. Because maybe, these people may not be paid themselves... This circle of "maybes" is a very strange one, Manto saheb. Believe me, anything can happen in this world...Rizvi can murder too.'

He fell silent. Naseer asked him, 'You were talking about Phaggu bhangi?'

Rizvi wiped coffee off his thin moustache with a handkerchief. 'Yes, I was. He may have been a thief, in the eyes of the law that is, but in my eyes he was completely honest. I swear to God, in all my life I haven't seen a man as honest as him. It's true that he had stolen three and a half annas, and he had said so very clearly in court. "Yes, I have stolen," he said. "I don't wish to defend myself. I hadn't eaten for two days. Hunger forced me to put my hand in Kareem the tailor's pocket. He owed me five rupees...salary for two months. But huzoor, I wouldn't blame him. Many of his clients hadn't paid him either. Huzoor, I have stolen earlier as well. Once I had taken ten rupees from a memsahib's purse. I was jailed for a month. Then I had stolen a silver toy from the Deputy saheb's house, because my child had pneumonia...and the doctor wanted a big fee... huzoor, I'm not lying. I am not a thief. Circumstances were such that I was forced to steal...and that I was caught. There are far bigger thieves than me out there... huzoor, I don't have a child anymore. My wife is also gone. But unfortunately, huzoor, I have a belly. If it died all my troubles would end. Please pardon me, huzoor..." But huzoor did not pardon him, and branding him a habitual thief, sentenced him to a year of rigorous imprisonment.'

Rizvi was speaking very informally. There was no effort, no pretense in what he was saying. It seemed like the words flowed from his tongue on their own. I was silent, smoking one cigarette after another and listening to him. Naseer addressed him again, 'You were talking of Phaggu's honesty?'

'Yes.' Rizvi took a beedi out of his pocket and lit it up.

'I don't know what is honesty in the eyes of the law, but what I do know is that I had killed with honesty... and I think that Phaggu had stolen three and a half annas with complete honesty. I can't understand why people associate honesty with goodness. In fact, now I have started questioning what is good and what bad. What can be good for you can be bad for me. What is considered good in one society can be bad in another: us Muslims, consider it a sin to let our hair grow in the armpits, whereas the Sikhs don't care about this. If growing this hair is actually a sin, why doesn't God punish them? And if there is a God, I would request him, for God's sake, to break these laws made by humans, destroy these jails made by man... He can make His own jails in the sky. God should punish these people in His court...if nothing else, at least it would all happen in His presence.'

I was deeply affected by Rizvi's speech. It was

his forthrightness that struck me most. When he would talk, it didn't seem like he was addressing us but rather, talking to himself. His beedi went out. Perhaps, a knot of tobacco was stuck in it. He tried lighting it five–six times. And when he failed, he threw it away and addressed me, 'Manto saheb, I will remember Phaggu all my life. You might say that I am sentimental, but I swear to God there is no place for sentiment here. He wasn't my friend...no, he *was*—because each time he proved himself to be one.'

Rizvi took out another beedi from his pocket but it was broken. I offered him a cigarette. 'Thank you, Manto saheb...I am sorry, I have been talking nonsense. I shouldn't have. But then, Masha Allah, you are—'

I cut him short. 'Rizvi saheb, right now I am not Manto...I am only Saadat Hasan. Please continue, I am listening with great interest.'

Rizvi smiled. There was a sparkle in his intoxicated eyes. 'You are very gracious.'

Then he turned to Naseer and asked, 'What was I saying?'

'You wanted to tell us something about Phaggu's honesty,' I reminded him.

'Oh, yes,' he lit the cigarette that I had offered. 'Manto saheb, he was a habitual thief in the eyes of the law. On one occasion, he had stolen eight annas for beedis and, while trying to escape, he had jumped over a wall and broken his ankle. His treatment lasted for nearly a year. But when in jail, each time Jarji, my partner-in-crime, would send twenty beedis through him, he would give every single one of them to me, sneaking them past the police. Although there is a hawk-eye on all prisoners who become approvers, Jarji, my fellow approver, had managed to befriend Phaggu and make him his confidante. He was a bhangi but his personality was fragrant. Initially, when he brought beedis from Jarji, I thought this bastard thief must surely have flicked some. But I discovered later that he was honest to the core. He had broken his ankles stealing eight annas for beedis...and yet, here in jail, where he had no way of getting any tobacco, he would bring all the beedis sent by Jarji as if they were jewels that belonged to me. And then after some hesitation he would ask me, "Babuji, at least give me one." And I would give him just the one beedi... Men are such scoundrels.'

Rizvi shook his head as if he was disgusted with himself.

'As I have mentioned earlier, there were many restrictions on me. This is always the case with approvers. But compared to me, Jarji was rather free. He had bribed his way to many concessions and perks. He would get clothes, he would get soap, he would get beedis too...he would even get money to give bribes in jail... There were only a few days left for Phaggu's term to end, when he delivered the beedis to me for the last time. I thanked him. He wasn't happy about his release. When I congratulated him, he said, "I'll be back here, babuji...a hungry man has no choice but to steal...just as he needs to eat. Babuji, you are a good person—you have been giving me so many beedis...I pray that you and all your friends are released. Jarji babu likes you a lot."'

'And, he was imprisoned for stealing only three and a half annas,' Naseer said to himself.

Rizvi, taking a sip of the hot coffee, remarked coldly, 'Yes... for stealing only three and a half annas. And even those are deposited in the treasury... God only knows what fires of hunger that amount can extinguish...' He took another sip and said to me, 'Manto saheb...there was only one day left for his release. I was in desperate need of ten rupees...I needed the money to bribe a sentry in the jail...I don't want to go into the details. With great difficulty I had managed to source paper and a pencil, and wrote a letter to Jarji, asking him to somehow send me those ten rupees. I sent him the letter through Phaggu. Phaggu was illiterate. He met me in the evening and gave me a letter from Jarji. There were bright red notes of ten Pakistani rupees in it. I read the letter and this is what it said:

Dear friend Rizvi, I am sending you ten rupees, but with a habitual thief. I hope you get it...as he is getting released tomorrow.

I read the letter, looked at Phaggu and smiled. I was thinking: if stealing three and a half annas had earned him a years' sentence, just how many years would he get for ten rupees?

Rizvi took his last sip of the coffee, and without taking his leave, walked out of the coffee house.

Haircut

'You have made my life miserable...may God take me and deliver me from this hell.'

'Why are you praying for your death? All of this will end if I die...I am ready to kill myself if you say so. There is an opium den right here. One tola would be enough.'

'Go then! What are you waiting for?'

'I am going! Get up, give me...I don't know how much a tola of opium would cost...maybe ten rupees. Give me ten.'

'Ten rupees?'

'Well, yes...after all, I am giving up my life. Ten rupees isn't a lot.'

'I can't. Does it have to be opium?'

'I could do with poison.

'How much will that cost?'

'How would I know? I haven't had poison before.'

'You know everything. Why pretend to be a fool now?'

'You're the one making a fool out of me. How would I know how much poisons cost?'

'But you know everything.'

'But I know nothing about you, even now.'

'And, that is because you've never thought about me.'

'Now, this is not fair...it has been five years. Tell me about a single day when I haven't thought of you.'

'Oh, stop it. You've been talking such nonsense every single day of these five years.'

'The truth is nonsense to you? Well then, what can I say...'

'Why don't you just say what you want to? When have you ever held your tongue?'

'Now, you're being nasty again.'

'It is you who says nasty things. Take the Quran in your hands and tell me...when have I ever said anything offensive to you in the last five years? I'll tell you who's offensive—your...'

'Why did you stop? Come on, say what you wanted to.'

'I don't want to say anything. Who can say anything to you? All you want is to hurt people, and they shouldn't even complain. I am sick and tired of such a life.'

'What exactly do you want? At least, tell me that.'

'I don't want anything.'

'Then what is the meaning of all these complaints?'

'You know very well what they mean. Why are you feigning ignorance? If there are complaints, there must be a reason.'

'And what might that be?'

'How should I know?'

'Now this is a strange logic—you rip up something and then darn it yourself. Why don't you clearly tell me? I don't understand where these daily squabbles will take us.'

'They will take us to hell!'

'But you'll have my company in hell too.'

'I'm certainly not going there.'

'Then, where will you be?'

'I don't know.'

'There is so much that you don't know...most of all, you don't know of my love for you, you haven't felt it till now. I don't understand...either I've been a miser in expressing myself, or you don't have the heart to understand my feelings.'

'How do you mean?'

'What do you mean how do you mean? Every day in the last five years...every single day... That's the proof of my love.'

'Cursed be such a love that leaves one fed up.'

'Who can get fed up of love?'

'My example is right before you.'

'This means that you accept that I love you.'

'When did I accept?'

'What you just said was acceptance.'

'May be.'

'Not maybe...it was. But you won't admit it. And that is because you are stubborn. I cannot understand the minds of women. They get scared when you love them and angry when you ignore them even a little.'

'What rubbish.'

'Why? Is it because it comes from the mouth of a very sincere husband?'

'Oh, let it be. I have seen your sincerity.'

'Well, if you've seen it, why don't you have faith in me?'

'Don't bother me. I am not feeling well...I don't like anything.'

'Don't you like yourself at least?'

'By God, no. Not today...'

'You'll like everything tomorrow?'

'I don't know...anything.'

'How strange is it that you know everything—and yet you don't know anything. Why don't you tell me clearly that you hate me?'

'Alright then. Hear it now—I hate you.'

'I'm very hurt to hear this... I've always taken care of all your needs.'

'But you did not take care of one thing.'

'What thing?'

'You are intelligent enough to understand this... why should I spell it out?'

'At least give me a hint.'

'I don't know how to play these games...'

'Where did you learn to talk like this?'

'From you.'

'From me? I'm surprised that you're accusing me of this.'

'You can be accused of everything.'

'For instance?'

'I can't give you examples. For God's sake, please end this conversation. I'm sick of it. I've already told you that I...'

'What?'

'Allah! Tauba! Please don't trouble me anymore...I am about to pull my hair out.'

'Here, my head is at your disposal...you can gladly pull out my hair.'

'You are very fond of your hair.'

'Humans are fond of everything that belongs to them.'

'But hair like this on a man's head is a beehive... I don't understand why you should abstain from a haircut.'

'Oh, I'm an abstinent sort...'

'Such lies! Only the day before you told me that you'd had a drink at a party.'

'Lahaul wala! I just had a glass of sherry.'

'Now what wretched thing is that?'

'Oh, it's a very harmless thing.'

'The things you say! Sometimes I fear I'll start talking like you.'

'As if you don't! You know, your father, *he* used to swear. He hurled the choicest abuses for everything.'

"I am warning you. Don't you say anything against my late father. You're being very vulgar.'

'How am I being vulgar?'

'I don't know.'

'You don't know, but you've already condemned me.'

'Well, what I want to know is why have you let your hair grow so much? It terrifies me.'

'That's all? Such a small matter, and you've made such a song and dance. I'm going...'

'Where?'

'I'm just going...'

'For God's sake, at least tell me! Or I'll kill myself.'

'I'm going to Nusrat Hair Cutting Salon.'

Gentlemen's Brush

This incident is about twenty years old. I must have been around twenty-two...or may be a year or two younger. When it comes to dates and years, I'm hopeless. Most of my friends at the time were also young, although they were much older than me.

We would all sit chatting away for hours inside Hafeez Painter's shop, which was next to Bijli Chowk in Hall Bazaar. I had pretty much given up on my studies by then. Mubarak too had chucked his job in some estate somewhere and come back to Amritsar. Hafiz the painter had had a tiff with his father and rented a big shop for himself where, before him, a Sikh communist used to sell gramophone records. The shop abutted the Khairdin Mosque and opened into Hall Bazaar, which was a good location: right in the middle of the bazaar and in the shadow of the mosque; the profane should always be subordinate to the sacred, after all. And that was the reason why Hafeez liked it so much. On one side, the azaan would begin, and on the other gramophone records would play. But this never caused a riot. Although the smallest of things routinely led to murders.

Muslim-Muslim and Muslim-Hindu fights due to gang rivalries, boy-loving gangsters and whore-mongering were common among young ruffians. These brawls would go on for a few days and then fizzle out. Just like the insects in summer, which manically spin cobwebs around themselves and then appear still, like corpses. But before you know it, as the weather turns favourable, they come back to life and start biting people again.

Amritsar is a strange city. All kinds of things happened there in those days—right from the catfights of the sweeper-women to arm-wrestling bouts with the government. There were all kinds of people too. Like the rascals who would burst small firecrackers, just for the thrill of scaring people to death. There were people who loved to terrorize others and there were those who loved peace. There were the pious and austere kind and there were criminals and scoundrels too. There were mosques and there were temples, and inside them happened as many sinful acts as virtuous deeds.

All the different streams of human life flowed together endlessly. Political movements rose and fell. Gangsters killed each other. Debates raged between Muslims and Qadiyans, in which many noted clerics and scholars participated. Droughts came and natural calamities happened. Terror was unleashed at Jallianwala Bagh and thousands—Muslims, Sikhs, Hindus—were killed mercilessly. But Amritsar remained as it was.

Though Hafiz Painter's shop rang at all hours of the day with talk of politics, and social and economic matters, it was just casual chatter. Actually, all of them were artists who were more interested in music. Someone would pick up the tabla, someone else the sitar, another man would start playing the sarangi and yet another would pick up the tanpura and start singing in Miyan ki Todi, Malkauns, Bhaagiri or some other raag.

Here bhaang was mixed, hashish smoked; and there were frequent rounds of alcohol. This was so because those were easy days. For just eight and half rupees, you could buy a full bottle of the best scotch whisky. Hafiz would shut the heavy doors of his shop and we would sit on chatais and take our sweet time imbibing the heady drinks. And then, around midnight, when all the other shops would shut down, our music sessions would begin.

Almost all the singers had flaunted their talent here, whether dazzling or somewhat modest. This was because it was a gathering of lively and energetic young men. It was all in good fun, no one really minded being teased or mocked.

One morning, around ten, I was crossing Hafiz's shop on my way to the chemist to buy medicine for my ears. Hafiz, with a small paintbrush tucked behind his ear, called out to me in a loud voice. As I turned, he pulled out the brush and signalled for me to come and listen to what he had to say.

I went up and stood at the entrance of his shop. 'What is it, Hafiz saheb?'

Sticking the brush back behind his ear, he said, 'So the thing is, my love, we'll have old songs today. Machchar Khan and Basey Khan will also be there, and there'll be that other matter... Come before six. I've already informed all our other friends. Although I haven't heard him but apparently the new generation really likes him. He is young himself. They say that

Khan saheb sings passionately like a lover, and never disappoints.

I was very happy to hear this. 'I'll definitely come. But who is this creature...this Machchar Khan? Will you make him sit under the mosquito net?'

Hafiz Painter burst out laughing. 'Arre no, no...it's just that he has this strange habit: as he descends from a high note when he's singing, he slaps his thigh hard. So everyone calls him Machchar Khan as if he weren't singing but killing blood-sucking mosquitoes.'

I told him, 'Okay, let's see this buffoonery too. But one thing is certain: he isn't likely to leave your art studio alive, if he fails to kill any mosquitoes tonight.'

Hafiz cackled and pulling out the brush from behind his ear, started painting a signboard. 'Go away now. Don't waste my time, I need to finish painting this.'

I left and got the medicine from the chemist. As I stepped out, I saw Sheikh saheb, a wealthy eminent of the city, who was standing just outside and talking to two other gentlemen. I greeted him. He, as was his habit, struck the electricity pole next to him with his walking stick. Reassured by the sound, he asked, 'So, Saadat...how have you been?'

I replied, 'Janaab, with your blessings, all is well.'

The gentlemen with whom Sheikh saheb was talking were jet black but the colour of their achkan was even blacker.

One of the two men he was speaking to was rather thin, almost emaciated, with very sharp features. As Sheikh saheb began to walk away, this piece of ebony flesh ran up and started brushing his coat very delicately. Sheikh saheb asked him angrily, 'What is it?'

In a thin voice, that ebony man replied, 'There were some hair, huzoor, and a little dust.'

Sheikh saheb thanked him and said, 'Okay. Come home tomorrow morning.' And then he took off towards Company Bagh, striking the electricity poles on the way with his stick as he walked.

The next day, I saw the dark man again. He was in the company of two Lalas at the Katra bazaar. He was busy painstakingly removing the smallest speck of dust and other offending bits from their already clean coats. Even that day he was in his black achkan. Black cloth attracts all kinds of dirt and dust, but even though I looked carefully, I could not see a single speck on it. I think, he wasn't only a coat brush for other gentlemen, he was his own brush too.

I ran into a friend of mine in the bazaar. I asked him, 'Who is that ebony man?'

He asked in wonder, 'What do you mean "ebony man"? I had heard of monkey men. Where did you dream up an ebony man?'

I replied sharply, 'Arre, this man who is walking ahead of us. You are a twit of the first order. Don't you even know that ebony is a kind of wood?'

'So is that a piece of wood walking in front of us?'

'Abey, no. Ebony is black. He is wearing a black achkan, and by the Grace of God he is quite dark himself, so I called him ebony.'

My friend laughed and said, 'Arre, don't you know him? His name is "Gentlemen's Brush".'

'That much I've gathered.'

'Then what more do you wish to know?'

I snapped, 'What is he all about? What is his profession?'

My friend smiled, 'He belongs to the caste of Rababis, those who play music in the Durbar saheb.* But he doesn't go there.'

'How come?'

'He has managed to find the company of the rich.

*Amritsar's Golden Temple.

He hangs around with them, always brushing their coats.'

'But how does he feed himself?'

'Well, he serves the rich as I said...besides, he sings very well.'

'Have you ever heard him sing?' I asked.

'No, but I've heard people raving about it.'

While we were deep in conversation, that ebony gentlemen's brush had walked far into the bazaar after the two Lalas, dusting their coats.

My friend also went his way after a while. He had some important work, otherwise I would have tried to find out more about that man.

It so happened that shortly afterwards, I had to go attend a public function with my brother-in-law (who was the Honorary Magistrate of Amritsar, and God knows what else). Now I don't quite remember the details, but I think the function was in honour of the new Deputy Commissioner. And there he was, the same man in the black achkan, orbiting around the rich and the famous of the city. And I'm not exaggerating, in just half an hour, he had identified every eminent man in the gathering and cleaned his coat with his slim, delicate fingers. He picked stray hair from the collars of some and the backs of others... and where he couldn't find anything, he took out his handkerchief and dusted the coats, and received thanks in return.

Gathering courage, he sidled up to the Deputy Commissioner saheb, and dusted his trousers. The DC was an Englishman; he thanked the Gentlemen's Brush from the bottom of his heart.

A few nights later, it was drizzling and we were sitting in Hafiz Painter's shop, sipping whisky and enjoying Mashooq Ali Photographer's singing, when suddenly the door opened and the Gentlemen's Brush appeared. Addressing us all he said, 'I was passing this way and I heard someone sing. Masha Allah, it was beautiful. I know it's bad manners for me to just walk in like this without an invitation...if I have your permission, could I join this gathering for a while?'

'Yes, yes, of course! Come have a seat.'

Mubarak said, 'It will be our pleasure. Please come sit beside me. You're a great singer yourself. Would you care to have something?'

What Mubarak meant was if he would like some whisky but the Gentlemen's Brush replied with great nobility, 'No, I am denied this blessing.'

On everyone's insistence, he began to sing. It was

Miyan ki Todi which he sang in such a sweet voice that everyone was in raptures. He asked permission to leave afterwards. As everyone was completely drunk by then, they had no idea that it had begun to rain heavily outside. It was only when the Gentlemen's Brush opened the door that someone asked, 'Huzoor, how will you go? It is pouring.'

A smile danced lightly on the lips of the ebony brush. 'Please don't worry. Lala Jagat Narayan, the one who sells blankets, his car will be here shortly to pick me up. Please don't disrupt your party. Thank you.'

He shut the door of the shop behind him.

When it had stopped raining an hour or so later, the mehfil ended and the gathering dispersed. When we stepped out, we saw that a man was lying face down on the ground. I went up to look carefully and screamed, 'Arre, this is that Gentlemen's Brush.'

Hafiz, who was staggering, slurred, 'To hell with those gentlemen...let us all go home.'

Everyone followed his advice. As I turned to leave, I saw the man who always wore a spotless black achkan and brushed the coats of the rich and famous, begin to stir. His achkan was completely covered in mud, but there was no one to clean it.

The Child

When Zubeida got married she was twenty-five years old. Her parents would've married her off the year she turned seventeen, but they hadn't been able to find a suitable match. Whenever the talks would near conclusion, something would go wrong and the wedding would not materialize.

Finally, when Zubeida turned twenty-five her father accepted the proposal of a widower. He was around thirty-five, perhaps older. He was self-employed; his own boss. He had a shop for wholesale clothes and would earn 500–600 rupees every month.

Being an extremely obedient girl, Zubeida accepted her parents' decision. And so, the wedding finally happened and she went to her married home.

Her husband, whose name was Ilmuddin, turned out to be a very loving and decent man. He would take care of all of Zubeida's comforts. While most people hungered for good clothes, Zubeida had heaps of them. She had 3B-quality lawn cloth worth 40,000, and bundles of full-length Chinese silks that had come to her laden on two horses.

She would visit her parents every week. One day, just as she crossed the threshold of their house, she heard a wail. She went in to discover that her father had had a heart attack and was no more.

Now, Zubeida's mother was left all alone. Apart from a servant, there was no one else in the house. Zubeida requested her husband for permission to bring her widowed mother to stay with them.

Ilmuddin said, 'There is no need to ask for permission. This is your house, and your mother is my mother too. Go, fetch her. I'll make arrangements to get her belongings.'

Zubeida was very happy. The house was quite big; two-three rooms were lying vacant. She went in a tonga and brought her mother home. Her things too arrived, as per Ilmuddin's arrangements. After some deliberation, a room was chosen for Zubeida's mother.

Zubeida's mother felt very obliged and was touched by her son-in-law's behaviour. It crossed her mind many times to give all her jewellery to him, worth thousands of rupees, to invest in his business. But she was a miser by nature.

One day she told her daughter, 'I've been here for ten months, and I haven't spent a single paisa from my pocket. Even though your late father left me ten thousand rupees...jewellery being separate.'

Zubeida was making rotis over the angeethi. 'The things you say, Ma.'

'I don't know or care. I would have given all of this money to Ilmuddin already, but I want you both to have a child, then I'll give it as a gift.'

Zubeida's mother always wondered why they hadn't had a child till now. They'd been married for nearly two years, but still there was no sign of a child. She took her to many hakeems, had her take many concoctions, powders and pills, but without any satisfactory results.

Finally, she took refuge in the prayers of pirs and fakirs, used spells, potions and remedies, and wore all kinds of amulets and sacred threads. But her wishes did not come true. After a while, Zubeida was fed up. So one day she finally told her mother, 'Forget about all this...if there is no child, so be it.'

Her ageing mother was hurt. 'Beta, this is a serious matter. I don't know what's happened to you... You don't even understand the importance of having a child. It is only a child that keeps the garden of life evergreen.'

Zubeida put the roti in the basket. 'What do I do? How is it my fault if I can't birth a child?'

'It isn't anyone's fault,' her mother said. 'All we need is one blessing from Allah.'

Zubeida had said thousands of prayers to Allah asking to be blessed with a child. But all her prayers had gone unanswered.

When her mother kept pestering her about having children every day, she began feeling as if she was a barren field in which no plant could grow.

She started having strange dreams at night. Dreams which made no sense at all. Sometimes she saw herself standing in a vast desert with a child as delicate as a flower in her arms. She threw it into the air with such force that it disappeared into the sky.

Sometimes she would see herself lying in a bed made out of the meat of tiny little children, alive and crawling.

Seeing such dreams over and over again, she lost

her mind. Her ears would ring with sounds of children wailing, and she would ask her mother, 'Whose child is crying?'

Her mother strained her ears for this sound. But when she couldn't hear anything, she said, 'There is no crying child...'

'Nahi, Ma...it is crying. In fact, it's crying so much it can hardly breathe.'

Her mother said, 'Either I've gone deaf or your ears are ringing.'

Zubeida became silent, but for a long time she could hear sounds of a newborn baby crying and mewling. She even felt that her breasts were getting heavy with milk. She did not mention this to her mother. But when she went to her room to rest for a bit, she lifted her kameez and found her breasts swollen.

The voices of crying children kept dripping into her ears, but she had understood that this was all an illusion. The reality was that her heart and mind were being perpetually hammered with the question of why she couldn't have a child, and she herself felt this emptiness intensely, an emptiness that no married woman should know.

Zubeida became depressed. When the neighbourhood kids made noise, her ears felt like they would explode. She felt like stepping out and strangling all of them. Her husband Ilmuddin was not worried much about having children. He was caught up in his business. The price of cloth kept rising with each passing day. Since he was an intelligent man, he had already stored piles of cloth in his shop. Now, his monthly income had doubled.

But this rise in income did not give Zubeida any happiness. Every time her husband gave her a wad of notes, she would place it in her lap and sing lullabies to it. Then she would settle it into an imaginary cradle.

One day Ilmuddin found the wad of notes he had given to his wife lying in the milk vessel. He was very surprised and wondered how they got there. Finally, he asked Zubeida, 'Who's put these notes in this vessel?'

Zubeida replied, 'The children are really naughty. They must have done this mischief.'

Astonished, Ilmuddin asked, 'But there are no children here?'

Zubeida was far more astonished than her husband, 'Why, don't we have children here? Oh, the things you say...they must be returning from school any minute now. I will find out who's responsible for this mischief.'

Ilmuddin finally understood. His wife was losing her mental balance. But he did not mention this to his mother-in-law, as she was very weak.

In his heart of hearts, he mourned for Zubeida's mental condition. But her treatment was not in his hands. He consulted many friends. Some advised him to put her in the lunatic asylum. But just the thought of that terrified him.

He stopped going to the shop. He stayed home all the time and cared for Zubeida, lest she end up doing something terrible.

Ilmuddin's constant presence at home improved Zubeida's health to an extent, but she was very worried about who was running his business. What if the man he had put in charge of the shop was cheating them?

Thus she repeatedly asked her husband, 'Why don't you go to the shop?'

Ilmuddin lovingly replied, 'Sweetheart, I'm tired of working. Now I want to rest for a while.'

'But who is in charge of the shop?'

'I have a helper. He does all the work.'

'Is he honest?'

'Yes, yes, he's very honest. He keeps account of every paisa. Why do you worry?'

Zubeida replied with grave concern, 'Why shouldn't I worry? I have my children. I may not care about myself but I do worry about them. If this servant of yours runs off with your money, then your children...'

Tears came to Ilmuddin's eyes. 'Zubeida, Allah will take care of the children. But my servant is very loyal and honest. You shouldn't worry yourself.'

'I am not worried about anything. But there are certain times when a mother *has* to think about her children.'

Ilmuddin was very anxious about what to do. Zubeida would spend all day stitching clothes for her imaginary children, washing their socks, knitting them sweaters. Many times, she asked her husband to bring tiny sandals of various sizes, which she would polish every morning.

Ilmuddin would watch all this and his heart would weep. He thought that perhaps he was being punished for his sins. Although what these sins were, he had no idea.

One day, Ilmuddin met a friend who was very distressed. When Ilmuddin asked him why he was distressed, he said that he had had an affair with a girl and she was now pregnant. They had tried all possible methods of abortion but they had not been successful.

Ilmuddin said to him, 'Listen, don't try this abortion stuff...let the child be born.'

His friend, who had no interest in this child, said, 'What will I do with the child?'

'Give the child to me.'

There was some time for the child to be born. In the meanwhile, Ilmuddin convinced Zubeida that she was pregnant and would deliver after a month.

Zubeida repeatedly said, 'I don't want too many children. Don't we have enough already?'

Ilmuddin remained silent.

When his friend's lover finally delivered a boy, Ilmuddin placed him beside his sleeping wife. Waking her up he said, 'Zubeida, how long will you keep sleeping? Look...what is this by your side?'

Zubeida turned around to find a little child next to her, kicking its hands and feet in the air. Ilmuddin said to her, 'It's a boy. Now by the Grace of God, we have five children.'

Zubeida was very happy. She asked, 'When was he born?'

'At seven in the morning.'

'And I didn't have a clue! I think I must've passed out from the pain.'

'Yes...something like that. But by the Grace of God, all is well now.'

The next day, when Ilmuuddin went to see his wife he found her bleeding profusely. She had his cut-throat razor in her hand. She was slashing her breasts.

Ilmuddin snatched the razor from her hand. 'What do you think you're doing?'

Zubeida looked at the baby lying next to her and said, 'He wept the entire night...but my breasts had no milk. What a curse upon...'

Beyond that she could say nothing. She put one blood-soaked finger to the mouth of the child, and fell into an eternal sleep.

Meerut's Sharp Wit

Our hearts and minds had nearly recovered from the trauma caused by the failure of *Chal Chal Re Naujawan*.* Gyan Mukherjee had been busy writing a propaganda story for Filmistan for a while. Prior to writing the story and getting it approved, he had signed the contract with Nalini Jaywant and her husband Virendra Desai, whom she has divorced now, probably for Rs 25,000. The contract was for a period of one year. Mr Sashadhar Mukherjee, the Production Controller, had already spent ten months thinking and planning for the film. The plot of the story was so convoluted that it could never be finalized. After a hundred difficulties, somehow, an outline came into being. Gyan Mukherjee packed this outline in his leather bag and left for Delhi, so that by adding a few

*A film directed by Gyan Mukherjee which was released in 1944.

more things verbally, he could get it passed from the powers-that-be.

The plot was passed. When the time for shooting came, Virendra Desai demanded that his contract be renewed for another year, as the first contract was about to lapse. Rai Bahadur Chunnilal, the Managing Director, was a stubborn man. This resulted in a court case, and the verdict was declared in favour of Virendra Desai and his beautiful wife Nalini. In this manner, the propaganda film which only had an unfinished plot till now, was already under the burden of Rs 25,000. Rai Bahadur was in a hurry for the film to be ready, as a lot of time had been wasted. Quickly, Wali Saheb was called and a contract was signed with his wife, Mumtaz Shanti, and an advance of Rs 14,000 paid to her in black. That is, without a receipt.

Shooting happened for two days for a short scene between Mumtaz Shanti and Ashok Kumar, which was filmed after much nitpicking. When the bit was shown on screen, everyone disliked Mumtaz Shanti. This dislike was also caused by the fact that Mumtaz Shanti came to the set in a burqa and Wali Saheb had clearly told Mukherjee that no one would be allowed to touch her. This resulted in the removal of Mumtaz Shanti from the film, on the pretext that she wasn't suitable for the character she had to play. There would be many scenes where the heroine would have to expose parts of her body. It was a small episode but another 14,000 were lost. Now the incomplete plot of the story was buried under Rs 39,000.

Rai Bahadur Chunni Lal was infuriated. As it is the failure of *Chal Chal Re Naujawan* had put the company in a precarious state. Life was tough after taking loans from the Marwaris. Rai Bahadur's distress was understandable.

One day, Vacha, Pai, Ashok and I were sitting in chairs outside the studio, discussing these stupid actions of the company, because of which so much time and money had been lost. Ashok revealed to us that the 14,000 that Rai Bahadur had given to Mumatz Shanti had been actually borrowed from him. Ashok disclosed this in such a manner, scratching his dark calves, that all of us burst out laughing. But then we stopped suddenly.

On the gravel path in front of us, an unknown woman was heading towards the make-up room along with our hefty hairdresser. Duttaram Pai parted his black, fat and ugly lips, showing his frighteningly crooked and dirty teeth. Elbowing Vacha in the ribs, he addressed Ashok, 'Yaar, who is she?' Vacha slapped him on the head, 'Saale, who are you to ask?' As Pai got up to strike back, Vacha grabbed his wrist, 'Sit down, idiot. Don't go there. Just one look at your face and she'll run off.'

Pai was left gnashing his crooked teeth. Ashok, who was silent till now, said, 'Good looking hai.' For a moment, I looked at that woman carefully and said, 'Yes, she doesn't let the eyebrows cross.' Ashok did not understand. 'What does not cross?' I laughed. 'What I meant was that woman who just crossed us, she is easy on the eyes. She is pleasant-looking, but rather short.'

Pai again bared his ugly teeth. 'Arre, she will do. Won't she, Vacha?' Instead of Pai, Vacha turned to Ashok, 'Dadamoni, do you know who she is?'

'I don't know much,' Ashok replied. 'All I heard from Mukherjee was that someone was coming for a screen test today.'

The camera and the sound tests were done. We saw the rushes and gave our feedback. Ashok, Vacha and I did not like her at all, because her body language was very stiff. All of her movements were forced. Even her smile wasn't very attractive. But Pai had been bowled over by her. So, baring his ugly teeth, he said to Mukherjee, 'Wonderful screen face hai.' Duttaram Pai was a film editor, a master at his job. Since Filmistan was a place where people from all walks of life had the freedom to opine, Duttaram Pai would impart his wisdom to us from time to time—and he would get especially annoyed by my mocking it.

We had given our verdict. But S. Mukherjee chose that woman only, whose name was Paro, for a role in the propaganda film. So Rai Bahadur Chunnilal immediately signed her on a contract for a modest monthly salary. Now, Paro started coming to the studio every day. She was a very pleasant courtesan who got along with everyone. She belonged to Meerut, where nearly every rich man with colourful propensities was fond of her. Those people used to call her 'Meerut's Sharp Wit' because she would cut, and cut through very fine. She was rolling in money but she wanted to be in films, and this had brought her to Filmistan.

When the opportunity arose to speak freely with her, I got to know that Hazrat Josh Malihabadi and Mr Sagar Nizami* also used to frequent her establishment and listen to her singing. Her speech was refined, along with her skin, which impressed me greatly. Her bare arms, in small-sleeved blouses, looked like elephants' tusks—white, firm, and beautiful. Her fair skin had the kind of shine which comes from scrubbing sandpaper over wood. She would come to the studio in the morning, freshly bathed, all clean and bright, draped in a white or light-coloured sari, as if out of some soap advertisement. When she left in the evening she would be spotless, despite the clouds of dust and smoke throughout the day. She would be as fresh as she was in the morning.

By now Duttaram Pai was even more enamoured by her. As shooting hadn't started yet, he had all the time in the world, most of which he would spend chatting with Paro. I don't how she could tolerate his crass jokes, crooked teeth and his uncut, dirt-filled nails. I suppose that if a courtesan is to tolerate some thing, she can tolerate most things.

The plot of the propaganda film was handed over to me, to look at critically and suggest revisions and

*Both Malihabadi and Nizami were eminent Urdu poets of the time.

cuts. I looked at it and came to the conclusion that almost nobody could fix such a disjointed plot. There was no head or tail to it. However, this was a test of my capabilities, so I readied a new plot with great sincerity and hard work. Moreover, the directorial responsibilities, on my insistence, were going to go to Vacha, my close friend. So when the new plot was presented to the full bench of Filmistan I felt like a criminal awaiting a sentence.

S. Mukherjee gave his verdict in these few words, 'It is alright but has a lot of scope for improvement.' When Gyan Mukherjee was asked he pursed his lips, as was his habit, and said, 'Almost alright.' His Majesty was the same person who was known as the director of all the films directed by S. Mukerjee, although he had actually never in his life directed even one foot of film.

The thing is, at Filmistan the way of functioning itself was strange. You might direct the whole film but my name would appear on the screen. It might be my story but you might be called the writer. Everyone there would work together. You can understand this from how Duttaram, who had no clue what a film story was, used to give me advice. The difficulties of writing for a propaganda film can only be understood by someone who has written such a story. My biggest problem was including Paro in it, keeping in mind her looks, her short height and lack of acting skills. In any case, after a lot of brainstorming all hurdles were resolved. The story was fine-tuned and the shooting began.

After discussing amongst ourselves, we decided that Paro's scenes should be filmed right at the end, so that she could get more familiar with the ambience of a film set and shed her inhibitions about being in front of the camera. Whatever scene was to be shot, she would be right there with us throughout. Duttaram Pai had gotten so familiar with her that they were cracking jokes by now. I found Pai's flirting very off-putting and made fun of Paro in her absence. The bastard, with great stubbornness, would say, 'Saale, why are you jealous?'

As I have mentioned earlier as well, Paro was a very friendly courtesan who would talk to everyone. She met everyone in the studio, regardless of their position, with great warmth. So, she came to be accepted by all within a short span of time. The lower strata on the sets started calling her Paro Devi. The name caught on so much that the end credits of all her films read Paro Devi instead of Paro. Duttaram Pai took another step forward. With some trickery, he managed to reach her house one day. He sat there for a while, took full advantage of Paro's hospitality and went off. After that, he would land up there once or twice every week, faithfully.

Paro was not alone, a middle-aged man lived with her. He was twice her size. I had seen him with her a few times. He seemed less like a husband and more like her pimp. Pai talked about his meetings with Paro with such fervour in the canteen that we would laugh. Vacha and I made fun of him. But he was so stubborn that this did not affect him at all. Sometimes Paro would also be present when I made fun of his crude and ugly infatuation. But she didn't seem to mind and smiled through it all. I wonder how many hearts she had snipped in Meerut with that smile of hers.

She did not have the tackiness and crudeness of normal courtesans. She could be a part of civilized mehfils and lead sophisticated conversations. This was probably because her visitors in Meerut were not any riff-raff off the street. They included men who belonged to the rich and aristocratic classes. By now,

Paro was a familiar face in the studio and seemed very much at home.

It happens quite often in the film world: when a young girl or woman enters the industry, some man or the other promptly grabs her, as if she is a ball waiting to be struck by a bat. And all the players in the field pray that she will end up in their hands. But this did not happen with Paro. Maybe because compared to other film studios, Filmistan was a much cleaner place. Another reason could be that Paro was not in a mad rush to become a star.

Mohsin Abdullah (of the mysterious eyes), tired of his dry, celibate life, was trying to marry the Parsi girl Veera, whose life was as stark and plain as his. It was with this intention that he had stopped commuting with us in second-class, as Veera used to take the first-class coach. On top of all this, according to etiquette, he even had to hold her dog's leash in the train.

Even Laila's bitch was dear to Majnu, the Imam of all lovers.

Vacha was not interested in such charades. He had just managed to get rid of his nasty French wife after a lot of trouble. S. Mukerjee was in love with the angelic Naseem Bano. Gyan Mukherjee was completely out of the question. In my case, all I can say is that I really liked Paro's skin. One day I mentioned this to Shahid Lateef. He smiled and said, 'You like the cover, that's fine. But do you know what the book is like from the inside, what it is about?' Pai was a bigger butt of jokes by now, because once Paro had invited him over to her house and served him two pegs of Johnny Walker whisky herself. When he had got really drunk, Paro lovingly laid him down on her sofa. Now he was convinced that she too loved him, and since all of us had failed at winning her love, we were burning with jealousy. How Paro felt about all this, I don't know.

The shooting continued. Veera was the lead actress and Paro the second lead. She had to play a sharp and saucy girl from one of the tribes of Burma. As the days for filming her scenes approached, my doubts also increased. I feared that she would not rise to the occasion and cause us great anguish. Finally, it was Paro's first day of shooting. She was brought in front of the camera, all decked up in her costume and make-up. She was wearing an oddly shaped, tight and garishly coloured blouse, her navel and just a little bit of her stomach showing. Her lehenga was slightly above her knee.

Paro seemed absolutely comfortable and unafraid of the dazzling lights, cameras and mikes. She was made to learn her dialogues thoroughly. We hoped that she would deliver her lines but, when the time came for the first take, her whole being turned into wood. She couldn't utter a single word. When she did open her mouth, her lines fell flat. Despite many rehearsals on the spot, that piece of wood showed no signs of life. Like a seasoned courtesan, she would just move her eyebrows, as if quoting a price. After three–four retakes I was completely disheartened.

Vacha was one of those who would get worried very easily. When he saw there was no scope of her improving, he asked S. Mukherjee to coach her. But what could Mukherjee do? She was made of such clay that all she had were airs and affectations. So when in one take she managed to do some passable acting, Mukherjee took it as a blessing and accepted the shot. All of us made great efforts to rid her of the stiffness, but we were unsuccessful.

The shooting continued and she did not improve at all. She wasn't scared of the camera or the mike, but she was unable to summon any acting skills. What could be the reason behind this, but the mujras of

Meerut? Anyhow, there was hope that finally some day she would learn some acting.

Since I was quite disappointed in her acting, I started editing out her role. Paro learned about this shrewdness of mine through Pai. So she started coming to me in her spare time. She would sit for hours, chatting about this and that. She would praise me in a proper and sophisticated language, in a way that would not reek of flattery. She even invited me over to her house a couple of times. I would have probably gone, but I was very busy those days.

The screenplay of this propaganda film weighed heavily on my mind all the time. Although there were three more people to help me out—Raja Mehndi Ali Khan, Mohsin Abdullah and Dikshit. But Raja Mehndi Ali Khan refused to help me point-blank—he was perpetually busy writing letters to his upset wife. Mohsin Abdullah was busy advancing his relationship with Veera and Mr Dikshit would help Paro memorize her lines.

I kept noticing for some time that whenever Paro and Ashok came face-to-face on the set, and Paro had to express her on-screen love to Ashok, her eyes would bore straight into his, as if she wanted to tell him: listen, whatever is happening here, it is true and not make-believe. Ashok was a very shy person. He could not handle any woman's open declaration of love for him. I knew that he liked Paro, but I also knew that he didn't have the courage to start a physical relationship with her. Not hundreds, but thousands of girls had come into his life. He could have been Lord Byron but, because of his shy nature, he would run away from all those easy birds. This was the time in Ashok Kumar's life when he could lay his hands on any actress. In fact, many actresses themselves were ready to lay their hearts at his feet.

I was not surprised that Paro too had such feelings for him. Then again, she *was* a newcomer, and by attaching herself to Ashok, she could easily reach the heights of fame. In the film, Paro's role was that of a free-spirited tribal girl who was arrogant and aggressive in love. She loved Ashok but he had fallen for Veera. This filmy triangle provided the fuel for Paro's inflamed desire for Ashok.

The shooting continued, indoors and outdoors. One day, there was a scene involving boats, and a far-away creek was chosen for the filming. There were two boats: one had Ashok Kumar, the other

Paro. She was instructed to jump into Ashok's boat as they neared each other. The water was deep. As instructed, Paro jumped but the two boats floated away from each other, and she fell in the water. Vacha screamed for help and two–three fisherman from the shore immediately jumped in and dragged her out. Although she was a woman, it was surprising that this incident did not frighten her at all. She was ready for the next take the moment her clothes dried.

When she was wringing her wet clothes, Ashok and I caught a glimpse of her leg, which was quite something. Once we got done with shooting and were on our way home, Ashok said, 'Manto, the leg was so nice...I felt like making a roast and eating it up.' It is strange that a cowardly and shy person like Ashok would come up with such a thing. The only possible explanation could be that since he was used to suppressing his feelings so much, such baseness was bound to show up.

Ashok and I used to go home from the studio in his MG sports car, chatting about all manner of things. Each time, we would pass through the road leading to the lane of Paro's flat. One evening after we crossed that lane, Ashok stopped the car.

'What's the matter?' I asked him.

Ashok turned around and looked towards the lane. 'Paro is throwing a feast for Holi tonight...should I go or not?'

'Why should I have any objection? Go!'

'So then, come. You also come along.'

'Why should *I* come? She hasn't invited me.'

'That doesn't matter.' Saying this, he quickly turned the car around, floored the accelerator and only braked outside Paro's flat. When he honked, Vachha and Pai appeared on the balcony. When Pai saw me, he bared his ugly teeth and said, 'Arre, you have also come.'

Vachha invited Ashok, 'Come, Dadamoni, come... we were all waiting for you.' Paro was sitting inside, unusually decked up in a Banarsi sari, looking like a bride. When we entered the room she got up to receive us. Seeing me, she profusely apologized for forgetting my invitation.

The rounds of drink started right away. As we finished the first peg, Pai seemed to sway, and Vacha requested for a song or two. Paro, looking at Ashok out of the corner of her eyes, said, 'So Ashok saheb, will you listen to something?'

Ashok was mortified and in his peculiar, blunt way, just managed to say, 'If you sing, I will listen.'

The song began. It was a cheap thumri. There was a ghazal after that, and then a film song. All this while Paro's husband, or whoever he was, kept pouring booze and soda in the glasses. Pai was nodding off after the second peg. Ashok wasn't much used to drinking and couldn't go beyond one and a half pegs. Vachha covered his glass with his hand after three pegs. The thumris, ghazals and songs went on for a long time. Finally when she sang a bhajan, she realized my presence and started singing a *naat*,* but I stopped her immediately. 'Paro Devi, this is a lively gathering...alcohol is going around. It's best if we don't remember Krishna here.' She acknowledged her mistake and asked forgiveness.

The food was very good. Ashok finished eating quickly and Paro got up to help him wash his hands. When he returned from the bathroom after a few minutes, he seemed a bit disturbed. He wanted to leave as soon as possible, forcing me to go along with him. He said nothing on the way, dropped me home and left.

---

*A poem in praise of the Prophet.

Many days passed. The shooting was happening regularly. One evening, when Ashok and I were going back home, he slowed the car down near Shivaji Park, where Paro stayed, and said, 'Manto, can I tell you something interesting?'

There was a strange quiver in his voice. For a second, I wondered what it could be.

'Tell me.'

Ashok started laughing. 'Do you remember...the day we had gone to Paro's house for dinner...and she had got up to help me wash my hands?'

I remembered how Ashok had returned worried. 'Yes, yes!'

'In the bathroom, as she handed me the towel she whispered, "Come alone tomorrow, six-thirty in the evening." I got scared, threw the towel and came out.'

Ashok had now stopped the car by the side of the road.

'Did you go?' I asked.

'Yes!' Ashok took his hands off the steering wheel and started rubbing them furiously. 'But even from there I ran off.'

'What exactly happened? Tell me the whole scene!' I wanted all the details.

'I am a coward. I don't know what happens to me in these moments. She made me sit on the sofa, and sat down on the carpet next to me. She made me two pegs, and drank some herself. And then she started professing her love for me. I kept listening, and trembling. When she pressed my hand, I got startled and shook it off with great force. Her eyes had welled up with tears, but then they suddenly disappeared. She started smiling, "Bhaiyya Ashok, I was only testing you."

'I was flabbergasted when I heard this . As I got up, she continued, "Ashok saheb! I think of you as my brother." I didn't say a word, and came downstairs. I sat in the car, got home, and after half a peg thought, what a shame. What was the harm if I...?' There was great remorse in Ashok's voice.

'Yes, there was no harm,' I said, and Ashok seemed even more crestfallen.

'And I liked her too...'

Hearing this, I recalled the scene which was being filmed every night at nine o'clock, in the extreme cold outside the studio. People dancing and singing in joyous celebration, Ashok lost in the arms of his heroine, Veera...and Paro standing to one side, alone in her melancholy.

Women of Prey

Today, I will tell you stories of some women of prey. Perhaps you've also come across them at some point.

I was in Bombay. I would usually take the early evening train from Filmistan* and reach home by six. But I got late that day. And, that was because of a prolonged discussion on the story of *Shikari*.**

When I got off at the Bombay Central station, I noticed a girl who was coming out of the third-class compartment. She was fairly dark. Her features were alright. Her gait seemed unusual...as if she was rehearsing a film scene.

---

* A film studio founded by Ashok Kumar, Shashadhar Mukherjee, Rai Bahadur Chunilal, Ashok Kumar and Gyan Mukherjee after they left Bombay Talkies.

**A film written by Manto which was released in 1946.

Exiting the station, I waited for the Victoria.* As I am used to walking fast, I had come out much before the other passengers. The Victoria arrived and I hopped in. I asked the coachman to go slowly as I was feeling rather unwell, because of the prolonged discussions at Filmistan. It was a pleasant evening. The coachman began to steer the Victoria down the bridge.

When we reached the main road, I saw a man carrying a matka covered with a sackcloth on his head, calling out, 'Kulfi...kulfi...'

I don't know why, but I asked the coachman to stop, and asked the man selling kulfi, 'Give me one.' I guess I just wanted to feel better and thought it would help.

He gave the kulfi in a little leaf-cup. I was about to have it, when someone suddenly hopped onto the Victoria. It was dark...but I could tell she was the same dark-complexioned girl.

For some reason I felt quite nervous. She was smiling. The kulfi began to melt.

Very casually, she said to the kulfiwala, 'Give me one as well.'

---

*A horse-drawn carriage, popular in Bombay at the time.

He gave her one.

That dark-complexioned girl finished it off in a minute and asked the coachman to continue.

'To where...?' I asked her.

'Wherever you want...'

'I have to go to home.'

'Then let's go home.'

'But who *are* you?'

'You pretend to be so innocent.'

I now understood what kind of a girl she was. I said to her, 'It won't be appropriate to go home...and this Victoria too isn't right. Let us take a taxi.'

She seemed very pleased with this suggestion. But she didn't move. I couldn't figure out how to get rid of her. If I pushed her out of the Victoria, there'd be quite a scene. Besides, being a woman, she might take advantage and cause a ruckus, saying that I had misbehaved with her.

The Victoria kept moving and I continued to worry about how to get rid of this problem. Finally, we reached the taxi stand near Bibi Hospital. I paid off the coachman and hired a taxi. We both got in.

'Where do you want to go, saab?' the driver asked.

I was sitting in the front seat. After thinking

for a while, I whispered to him, 'I don't need to go anywhere... Here, take these ten rupees...and take this girl wherever you like.'

He seemed very happy.

Stopping the car at the next turn, he said to me, 'Saab, you wanted to buy some cigarettes...you can get them cheap at this Irani's hotel.'

I quickly leapt out of the car.

The girl called out, 'Get two packets!'

'He will bring three,' the driver said and, restarting the engine, took off like the wind.

~

This is another incident from Bombay. I was alone in my flat—my wife had gone out shopping—when a sharp-featured ghaatan confidently walked in. I assumed that she must have come looking for some domestic work. But she came and sat on a chair, took a cigarette out of my cigarette-case, lit it and smiled at me.

I asked her, 'Who *are* you?'

'Don't you recognize me?'

'I am seeing you for the very first time.'

'Saala! Don't you lie...you see me every day.'

I was in a fix. But just a short while later, my servant Fazaluddin arrived. He took this sharp-featured woman in his charge.

~

This incident is from Lahore.

A friend and I were going to the radio station. When our tonga crossed the Assembly Hall, another tonga overtook ours. There was a burqa-clad woman in it, whose face was half-covered.

When I looked at her I saw a strange mischief in her eyes. I told my friend, who was sitting in the backseat, 'I think that woman is characterless.'

'You shouldn't judge so quickly.'

'Very well, janaab...I will be more cautious in the future.'

The tonga of that burqa-clad woman was a little ahead. She kept staring at us. Although I am a big coward, I had a naughty idea that day. I bowed my head and wished her aadaab.

I was rather disappointed when I saw no reaction on her half-covered face.

My friend started giggling. He was very pleased with this failure of mine but when we reached Shimla

Pahadi, the burqa-clad woman stopped her tonga. And (I won't go into the details), smiling under her half-raised naqaab, she climbed into our tonga and sat next to my friend.

I did not know what to do now. I didn't say a word to the burqa-clad woman, and asked the tongawala to take us to the radio station.

When we reached, I took her inside. I was on friendly terms with the Director. I told him, 'We found this lady on the road. I have brought her to you, and I request you to find her some work here.'

He got her voice tested and seemed very satisfied with the result. When she returned after her audition, her burqa was off. I observed her closely. She might have been around twenty-five years old. Fair, big eyes. But her body looked like an ash-roasted sweet potato.

The peon came while we were talking. 'There is a tongawala standing outside. He is asking for his fare,' he said. I assumed that he must have got annoyed waiting for so long, so I went out to see for myself. I asked my tongawala, 'What is it, bhai? I wasn't running away.'

He seemed very surprised, 'What are you saying, saab?'

'Didn't you send for your fare?'

'No, saab. I didn't send anyone.'

There was another tonga parked behind ours. The coachman of that tonga was feeding hay to his horse. He came up to me and asked, 'Where is the woman who had gone with you?'

'She is inside. Why do want to know?'

'Well, she has wasted two hours of mine! Just asking me to go here and there...I don't think she even knows where she wants to go.'

'So, what do you want now?'

'All I want is my fare, saab.'

'I will bring her.'

I went inside and said to that burqa-clad woman, who was no longer in a burqa, 'Your tongawala is asking for his fare.'

She smiled and replied, 'I will give it.'

I picked up her purse, which was lying on the sofa. When I opened it, I saw that there wasn't a single paisa in it. There were a couple of bus tickets, two hair clips and one cheap lipstick.

I didn't think it was appropriate to say anything in front of the Director. Taking his permission, I stepped out and paid the tongawala for the two hours. Back inside, in the presence of my friend I told that woman, 'You should have at least been aware that you had hired a tonga, and didn't have a single rupee on you.'

She got sheepish. 'I...I...you are a good man.'

'I am bad...but you're a good woman. Come to the radio station from tomorrow...it will be a way to earn money. End the other nonsense that you have started.'

I dropped her near Mozang* and went home. My friend also went his way. By chance, shortly afterwards, I had to go back there for some work. As I got there I spotted my friend and that woman going off some place together.

~

This too is an incident from Lahore.

A few days ago, I forced my friend to lend me ten rupees. The banks were closed that day and he expressed his inability to do so. But when I pressed him to produce the ten rupees any which way and told him that I had to satiate my addiction, of which he was well aware, he said, 'Okay...I have a friend who

*A place in Lahore.

might be in the coffee house at this time. He might be able to help us.'

Both of us got onto a tonga and started towards the coffee house. On Mall Road, a tonga was crossing the big post office. A woman in a brownish burqa was sitting in it. Her face was not covered at all, and she was chatting with the tongawala with great familiarity. We couldn't hear her, but I could figure out what I needed to know, merely from the movement of her lips.

As we reached the coffee house that woman's tonga also stopped there. My friend went inside and managed to arrange for the ten rupees. The woman in the brown burqa stayed outside, waiting for someone.

On our way back home, we spotted piles of muskmelons being sold. Both of us got down the tonga and began inspecting the fruit. Unanimously we decided that the melons would not turn out well as they looked misshapen. When we rose to leave, we found the brown burqa sitting in a tonga, considering the melons.

I whispered to my friend, 'Melons take the colour of the melon they look at. You don't appear to have caught this shade of brown yet.'

'Oh, come off it…all of that is nonsense.'

We got up and sat back in our tonga. My friend had to stop at a chemist nearby, which took us about ten minutes. When we came out of the shop, the tonga with the brown burqa went slowly past us.

My friend was very surprised. 'Now, what is this? Why is this woman roaming around aimlessly?'

'I am sure there must be a reason,' I said.

As our tonga was about to turn towards Hall Road, we again spotted that brown burqa. Although my friend is single, he is also very pious. I don't know what provoked him to shout out loudly to the brown burqa, 'Why are you wandering around like a vagrant? Come, join us.'

Her tonga turned and my friend got pretty scared. When that brown burqa came face-to-face she remarked, '*You* don't need to be a vagrant roaming around in a tonga. I am ready to marry you.'

And my friend married that brown burqa.

Sitara

Although I have crossed many milestones as a writer, I find myself hesitant and uncertain as I sit down to record my impressions of the famous dancer and film star, Sitara. Most of you know her only as an actress who dances, and makes others dance to her tune. But I have had the opportunity to study her character, which is extremely strange.

I have studied the personality and behaviour of many women, but as I slowly became aware of the circumstances of Sitara's life, I was dumbfounded. She is not a woman but a storm—a recurring storm that will rage on till eternity. While she appears slightly built, she is an astonishing powerhouse. Had any other woman had to weather as many illnesses as Sitara has weathered, she would not have survived. She is naturally brave and daring—perhaps because of all the exercise she does.

I have seen her get up early every morning to practice dance for at least an hour, and believe me, it is no ordinary practice. An hour of rigorous dancing can be bone-crushing, but Sitara never seemed to tire. She had vast quantities of what is called stamina in English; she isn't of a species that knows exhaustion. Things that would defeat everyone else, Sitara accomplished without even breaking a sweat. I think it was because she loved her art intensely. She loved it as fiercely as she loved her men.

Sitara puts in more work for a single dance routine than any other artiste might do for a lifetime of dancing. That's just how she is—temperamentally incapable of doing the usual. She's full of restless energy; every cell in her body dances even when she is still.

It is said that she comes from Nepal. I don't know much about that, but I can confirm that she had two sisters. Together they were a female Trinity—Tara, Sitara and Alaknanda. Tara and Alaknanda have disappeared from the scene; I doubt anyone even remembers their name.

All three sisters have had interesting lives. Tara has been involved with many men. In this multitude was a chancer called Shaukat Hashmi, whose wife Poornima divorced him recently and he has been sharing the painful details with the whole world. Alaknanda also passed through many hands, finally reaching the famous Prabhat Film Company actor Balwant Singh. I don't know if she is still with him or has moved on.

If I were to attempt a full and honest biography of these sisters, I could fill up thousands of pages. People accuse me of being obscene and vulgar. But they never stop to think that the world abounds with the strangest of specimens. I don't call them obscene. All I know is that human beings do what they do either because of their environment or some twisted natural impulse. Psychiatry may have a cure for a trait that we are born with, but who is to blame if we have no knowledge of this? It's something to think about.

Tara, Sitara and Alaknanda—where were they born? Perhaps in some non-descript village in Nepal. One by one they made their way to Bombay, to try their luck in the film industry. And it was sheer luck that Sitara alone became a shining star; the other two sisters sparkled for a bit and faded away.

As I have already mentioned, I hesitate to write

about Sitara in full detail. She is not a single woman but many. I cannot write of her numerous sexual liaisons in this brief article. In English, such a woman is called a 'nymphomaniac'. This is a special breed of women that has relations with not one but scores of men. Whenever I think of Sitara, I imagine a five-storey Bombay building with many flats and many rooms. She keeps several men in her heart at any given time. I know that when she came to Bombay, she got into a relationship with some Gujarati film director whose name I can't quite remember. He was some Desai, a scrawny, dull man, though he had many virtues. He was clever in his work, but luck was not on his side. Because he was stubborn, he was spurned everywhere. I had met him around the time when Saroj Film Company was still alive, although in reality it was a walking corpse by then. We became friends instantly, because he knew how to appreciate art and had an interest in literature. It was during this time that I got to know of Sitara, his wife, although she had already separated from him. Desai, however, didn't seem very upset about the separation. All I could gather from our conversations was that he couldn't quite handle Sitara. She was with some other man at the time but she would still come to be with Desai sometimes. Being a self-respecting man, he would meet her briefly and as soon as they were done, he would send her off with no attempt at civility.

According to Hindu custom, a woman cannot be divorced. Desai had married Sitara as per Hindu law, so she remained Mrs Desai even as she picked up and dropped many other men. At the time that I got to know her, she was entangled with Mehboob, who was well on his way to becoming a big star. Mehboob had cast her in one of his films, and they had begun to sleep together. My pen cannot quite describe this liaison, only Bibbo's—Ishrat Jahan's—tongue can. Apparently, once, when Mehboob had to go to Hyderabad for an outdoor shoot, he would religiously offer namaz at regular intervals, and make love to Sitara with the same regularity.

I am hesitant about writing all of this. Sitara is actually a 'case history'. Perhaps only a psychologist should write about her... There was a studio called Film City in Bombay. It was there that Mehboob had probably started making his film. In those days P.N. Arora, now a famous producer, was a sound recordist there. He was a hard-working young man, and Fazal Bhai, who was in-charge of Film City, had sent him abroad to learn the art of sound production. According to Diwan Singh Maftoon, editor of *Riyasat* in Delhi, while Director Mehboob and Sitara were carrying on with each other, Sitara hooked up with P.N. Arora as well.

As soon as Director Mehboob had completed the film, Sitara moved in with P.N. Arora—whether as wife or mistress, I can't be sure. But this wasn't the end of it. Around this time, a newcomer named Alnasir made an appearance in Film City (or some other studio where Sitara was working). He was a beautiful young man, who had just arrived from Dehradun after completing his studies. Fair and rosy-cheeked, he wanted to become a film star. As soon as he arrived, he landed a role in a film. Coincidentally, Sitara—flitting between P.N. Arora, Director Mehboob and her 'husband', Desai—was also cast in the same film.

I don't know if Sitara got friendly with Nazir before or after his first mistress—the Jewish actress, Yasmeen—left him and broke his heart. I am not sure of the circumstances in which Nazir and Sitara met, but I do know that in those days they were thick as thieves: Nazir was smitten by Sitara, and Sitara could die for Nazir.

I know Nazir very well. He is a coarse man, convinced that women have to be subservient. Let alone women, even the men who work for him have to deal with his abuses and threats. He is not a man but a demon, albeit an affectionate demon. He is my friend. Whenever he meets me, he showers abuses on me, instead of greetings. But I know that he is not a phony. His heart is full of love.

This genuine and affectionate man tolerated Sitara for many years. But it was because of his harsh temperament that Sitara did not have the courage to keep seeing her earlier lovers. But what is the cure for that woman who cannot be satisfied by a single man? After a while, Sitara started the same routine that she was used to—Arora, Alnasir, Mehboob and her husband—all were beneficiaries of her largesse. This took a heavy toll on the proud Nazir. He was the kind of man who, once settled in a relationship, would want to keep it going. But Sitara was from another planet. She was never satisfied, even with a man like Nazir.

I don't blame Sitara for this. Whatever happened, happened solely because of her nature. Nature has made her such that she'll always be the wine in every cup. She could not have gone against her nature even if she tried.

Yasmeen was a reasonable woman, a brilliant example of beautiful femininity. I clearly remember when she expressed her desire to live a settled, domestic life to Nazir. And Nazir, a man whom most people considered cold-hearted, gave Yasmeen permission to marry whosoever she pleased.

Yet, I fail to understand how Nazir and Sitara's physical relationship lasted for so long. I met Nazir once at Hindustan Cinetone. This was the time when the film industry was in a precarious state. Producers were millionaires one day, and paupers the next.

Hindustan Cinetone was earlier called Saroj Film Company. God only knows what it was called before that. I had written a story titled 'Keechad', and when I narrated it to Seth Nanu Bhai Desai, he had liked it very much. At that time, when the government had put many restrictions on the industry, I believe that no other producer would have had the courage to film this story. But Nanu Bhai was fearless. Although later he ran into financial difficulties and was helpless.

In that story, I had written the central character of a worker for Nazir, which he had liked. When he found out that 'Keechad' was not going to be made because of lack of funds, he said to Nanu Bhai Desai, 'Please give me the story. I'll sell whatever I have to film it.' But that day did not come. Nanu Bhai liked the story. So somehow, the funds were arranged. Dada Gunjal, a Gujarati, was the director of the film. The film was completed and released and while people praised it, I was not satisfied. But this story is not about me. All I'm trying to say is that it was during this time that Nazir had the desire to make a film of his own. This was also when Yasmeen was getting ready to leave him. Nazir was a master of his desire and remained determined to make his own film very soon. As far as I remember, his first film was *Sandesha*.

Then he made his second film, which I think was called *Society*. He cast Sitara in this film. It was clear that they had fallen hard for each other, and for a long time. But as far as I know, Sitara also frequented her older friends during this time. She would visit P.N. Arora quite often.

Let me tell you a funny story. I had to leave Bombay and go to Delhi, where I found a job at All India Radio. For about a year, I was unaware of the goings-on in the Bombay film world. One day,

I suddenly spotted Arora in New Delhi. There was a thick walking stick in his hand, and his back was bent double. The poor man had always been frail, but he seemed to be in bad shape that day. Each step he took was with great difficulty, as if he was barely alive. I was in a tonga and he was on foot; I think he had come out for a walk. I stopped my tonga, got off and asked him what the matter was. Why was he in such bad shape? Panting, with a wry smile, he said, 'Sitara. Manto, Sitara.' I understood everything. I suppose you should also have understood by now.

Here's another funny story. Alnasir, who is now fat and ugly, was very beautiful when he had first come to Film City. Very gentle, very fair and rosy-cheeked. He had the glow of the mountain air of Dehradun. I tell you, he was as beautiful as a woman. He had all the grace and poise of a beautiful young woman. After one and a half years in Delhi, when Syed Shaukat Hussain Rizvi called me back to Bombay, I met Alnasir at Minerva Movietone. He was standing right outside the gate. I was surprised—the rosiness of his cheeks had vanished, and his pants were hanging loosely from his frame. It seemed as if he had shrunk, shrivelled up. I asked him worriedly, 'My love, what have you done to yourself?' Bringing his mouth close to my ear, he whispered, 'Sitara...my love, Sitara.'

Wherever you turn, there's Sitara. I thought Sitara was born to turn men into weaklings. On the one hand there was P.N. Arora, an England-educated sound recordist, on the other there was this young man just out of school from Dehradun.

When I took him aside to enquire about the details, he told me that he had fallen into Sitara's orbit, which had resulted in his ill-health. When he realized that if he continued seeing her he would die, he got his tickets and left for Dehradun. He stayed there in a sanatorium for three months and regained some of his health. He even told me that during this period Sitara even wrote him long letters in Hindi, which he couldn't read. But their arrival would always leave him shaken. Again, he whispered in my ear, 'Manto saheb, she is an incredible woman.'

Sitara *is* actually an incredible woman. The kind who is one in a million. I know she has fallen dangerously ill many times. She has contracted diseases that any ordinary woman would not have survived. But she is so resilient that she has cheated death every time. One would think her dancing powers would be destroyed after so many illnesses, but she still dances like she did in her youth. Every day she rehearses for hours, gets oil massages from the masseur, and does everything that she has been doing for years. She has two servants in her house. A man and a woman. Generally, it is the man who is her masseur. And for the woman, all I can say is that she seemed to be such a bundle of stories that she could even patch up the sky. She always wore a fine muslin sari. It was so transparent that her sagging body would shimmer through it, becoming the cause of disgust for those saw her. She was a woman of few words, but she had a sharp eye. She must have been at least fifty-five years old, but she was agile and healthy like a young woman. Her hawk-like eyes saw everything.

When Sitara was alone—she never belonged to one person alone—her house was on Khudadad Circle. Whatever virtues and vices she had were also 'khudadad'.* Nazir, who is now with Swarnalata, is also a man of many virtues. He tolerated Sitara for a long time, but as I have already mentioned, that woman cannot belong to one man. So when he got fed up with her and finally realized that he could no

*God-given.

longer carry on with her, he folded his hands and said, 'Sitara, spare me, please. I can't bear the mistake I have made, please forgive me.'

Nazir also used to beat up Sitara. But she was not unhappy with him. Women like her find a particular kind of sexual pleasure from such violence. But for how long could these men beat them? Those poor souls would also get fed up after a while.

Now here is another part to this story, listen. During the time when Sitara was staying with Nazir, his nephew, K. Asif, was also there. He was a strapping young man, well-built and full of youthful energy. Perhaps he had never dealt with women before, and now, he had come to stay with his uncle. He was learning about the ways of the film industry from him. He held many hopes and aspirations in his heart. Now having come into the film world, he was seeing women, that too film actresses, from close quarters. He had probably seen what went on between his uncle Nazir and Sitara. This was also the time when K. Asif's youth was overflowing. A time when men would happily run into brick walls in their youthful passion. Sitara was definitely a brick wall that wanted to crash into someone.

At that time, Nazir used to live in the compound opposite Ranjit Film Studio. It was a filthy place. Nazir had a whole flat to himself. The office of Hind Pictures, which he had started, was also there. There were only two–three rooms. What privacy could there be? So the hungry, youthful Asif got the chance to witness every aspect of an intimate relationship between a man and a woman.

This was a new experience for the young Asif. It was quite astonishing. He had heard about the intimate details of marital life from his friends many times, but he had never been astonished. He knew that there was a bed, where eternal games determined by human nature were played between two humans. But whatever Asif's eyes had seen that one time, by accident, was completely different. It was so scary that every bone in his body had shuddered. He had seen dogs fighting many times, when they would barbarically get entangled with each other. Like those dogs, they pulled and tore, bit and scratched each other. His whole body shivered.

He concluded that love was a farce. In reality, humans are beasts and love is a frightful wrestling match. But he definitely wanted to enter the ring and take part in this wrestling. His arms had the strength. His body had the hunger. His muscles were like iron. All he wanted was to be given one chance, then he would overcome his opponent and pin her down.

Director Nayyar (an intelligent but unlucky director from Pakistan) was also working with Nazir at this time. Asif and Nayyar were of the same age. Both were bachelors and lived in their own dream worlds. When they got together they talked of women. The women who would be theirs in the coming future. But every time Sitara's name came up, both of them shuddered and were transported to the world of jinns, gods and witches. How could they know what 'nymphomaniac' women were like? How could they know, that besides Sitara, there were also women who could be called slabs of ice, and rightly so. What they did know was that Sitara was not faithful to Nazir. She was a wanderer. Although she lived as Nazir's 'whole-time' mistress, she also went to P.N. Arora, and sometimes to her husband Desai, the poor man who spent his days in poverty. Then there were more, like Alnasir.

Both of them, Asif and Nayyar, remained dazed. They were unable to fathom anything. They knew about the wrinkles on Nazir's bed. They knew why there were spots and scars on his thick-skinned, rough and dark face. They were also sure that this thing would not last for long—but they were wrong, and it went on.

Sitara would get up early in the morning and start her practice in the other room. Even this sight was quite incredible—from the moment she got up, she would dance for two hours non-stop, like a courtesan. She would spin so fast that the floor would be in a tizzy and the tabla player's hands would go numb. But she remained unfazed. After practice, she would get a massage from her special masseur. Then after bathing, when Nazir was still sleeping, she would go into his room. She would wake him up, force some milk—or God only knows what was in that cup—down his throat, and then another dance would begin. All of this happened right in front of Asif and Nayyar's eyes.

Theirs was the age of curiosity, a time when a man would peep through holes even into an empty room. The slightest of sounds would perk up his ears, filling them with meaning, and he would slyly eye rooms with ventilators. Compared to Asif, Nayyar was physically very weak. So his sexual desires were moderate. But in his strapping, athletic body, Asif's veins were brimming with an electricity that demanded a conductor. He dreamt of a dark night thronging with black clouds and ear-splitting thunderstorms, so he could drag someone with his firm hands to a rocky bed.

Since he was close to Nazir, Sitara would sit with Asif for hours and chat about all manner of things. As time passed, Asif's inhibitions, which he had brought from Lahore, seemed to end. Still, he could not muster enough courage to touch her as he was afraid of his uncle. Although he did know, by now, that Sitara was attracted to him. He knew that he could, at any time, take her wrist in his strong hand and go wherever he wished. That pitch-dark and stormy night, that rocky bed...

It was maddening for Asif—he wondered why nature was taking so long. Whatever has to happen, why can't it happen today? Trains which have to crash into each other tomorrow, why can't they crash into each other today? But how could anything happen, if the person who has to shift the gear does not make a move?

Both of them would halt at the same platform like

two trains, though the gap between them remained. It was a small gap, but just like two trains chained to their tracks, they could not meet. They could talk to each other as passengers from one train stick their heads out to speak with passengers on the other train. But soon, one train would go here, the other there. Asif would get infuriated, but he continued to wait for the dark and stormy night.

Then that dark and stormy night, mixed with the terrors of thunder and lightning, finally came. Nazir was shocked at seeing this deed of Sitara's.

He had reached the end of his tether. After a lot of yelling and cursing, he told Sitara that she couldn't stay with him any longer, and she had to pack up her things and leave.

Whatever she might have been, Sitara was still a woman. After hearing so much from Nazir, she did not have the strength to pack her bedding by herself. But how could she ask Nazir for help? He had left foaming at the mouth, seething with anger, and gone and sat down in his office. When Asif saw him in this state, he was sure that the dark night had come.

Asif sat silently for a while. Then he got up and slowly crept into the other room, where Sitara was sitting on the bed, nursing her wounds. In a few words he got to know that the relationship was over. Privately, he was very pleased. So he consoled Sitara in such a way that a new affair began.

He packed her things and went to drop Sitara to her place in Dadar (Khudadad Circle). She thanked him profusely. Asif mustered some courage, grabbed her hand and said, 'You don't have to thank me, Sitara...'

Sitara did not try to free her hand from Asif's grip. But Asif was not satisfied with this. For a while, they whispered sweet-nothings to each other. Sitara even gave him a taste of her magic, with which she had enslaved hundreds of men—frail, strong, stubborn and wild.

Had it been daytime, Asif would have surely glimpsed the stars. But from that flat on Khudadad Circle, he saw the sun rising in that dark night. It had been a day of bliss for him, but somehow, he was still not satisfied. He told Sitara, 'Listen, our relationship should be strong. Forget your harlotry, just be with me.'

Sitara assured Asif that she would not even look at anyone other than him. Asif was placated, but afraid that Nazir might ask him why he was so late. So he kissed her hand like a true lover and left. He promised to return the following day.

Once he left, Sitara got up. She went up to the dressing table, fixed her hair, changed her sari and without another glance at anyone, went downstairs and took a taxi to P.N. Arora's house.

But all of that is another story. What I actually wanted to say was that Sitara hated me with a vengeance. I was the editor of *Musavvir* and wrote without bias. I had torn her apart many times in my 'Baal ki Khaal' and 'Nit Nayee' columns. But it was all civilized, there was nothing vulgar about it. Still, Sitara was upset with me. But to be honest, I did not really care. For one, I was not invested in pleasing her and secondly, I tried to stay as far away from film personalities as possible. When I spiced up her fight with Nazir in my columns, she was furious and showered many curses on me.

Later, when I found out about her secret affair with Asif through my spies, I hinted and insinuated the same in my columns. This angered her so much that she asked Asif, 'Why won't you beat this man up? If you can't beat him up yourself, you should get him thrashed by someone else, or get someone in the media to abuse him in their newspaper.'

Asif is a large-hearted man. He is decent, patient and has the ability to understand humour, even though he is illiterate. He heard Sitara's complaints from one ear and let them out the other.

The matter had become very delicate. You know by now the kind of woman Sitara was. Any man ensnared by her found it difficult to escape. Only Alnasir had managed to extricate himself and run off to Dehradun after a few months with her. Otherwise, his insides would have given up one day and he would have been buried in some graveyard in Bombay, with an epitaph that would have said—

They come covered in a veil to my grave,
May the morning breeze extinguish the poor lamp.

So, what I was saying was that the matter had turned very delicate because Nazir was getting suspicious about the long absences of his nephew, who in turn would have a new excuse every time he was questioned. But how long would these excuses have lasted? They had to run out some day.

There was no place for Sitara now in Nazir's heart. He was not the kind of man to go back on a decision.

It was Asif that he was worried about, not her. He had taken charge of his nephew because he loved him, and wanted him to amount to something.

So, his main concern was that he should not get involved with that woman. He had spent many years with her. He knew her inside out. He knew that Asif was just the kind of young man that Sitara would like. And for an experienced woman like her, it was not difficult to seduce him. What is amusing is that such youngsters would usually come under her spell all on their own. Once caught, getting free was next to impossible.

If Sitara came across a man and by chance, she took a liking to him, he would end up spending most days and nights with her. Nazir had figured it all out from Asif's regular absences. But every time he was confronted, Asif would deny the accusation, saying, 'Mamujaan, what are you saying? I can't even imagine doing something like this.' This would completely confound Nazir. But in his heart of hearts, he knew that the boy was hooked and was lying to him.

Asif *was* indeed lying. Had it been any other woman, he definitely would not have lied, but Sitara had been his uncle's mistress. He could not have such relations with her. The relations which had already happened.

There was no stopping and no going back now. Asif was firmly under the spell of that enchantress. There was no way he could escape. But on the other hand, Nazir's blood boiled with each passing day. He just needed one opportunity, so he could see everything with his own eyes.

One day, Nazir did see what he wanted to see with his own eyes. My memory is failing me now. I knew everything that had transpired, but so much has happened since then, I can't remember all the details. I know that all hell broke loose as Nazir finally unleashed all his wrath on the both of them.

Asif continued to swear to his uncle, trying to assure him that both of them were innocent. That there was no such relationship between them, of which they could be accused. But at that time Nazir did not wish to hear anything. It seemed that he wanted to thrash them both and break their bones, ending this whole sordid ordeal once and for all. But Majeed (the famous actor, who is now in Pakistan) very cleverly intervened and saved the situation.

Nazir agreed. Generally, he does not listen much

to anyone. But in those days, Majeed was, according to the English proverb, 'in his good books'. Majeed knew about the affair between Asif and Sitara. I have heard that he even warned Asif many times to stop playing such a dangerous game. But Asif, who was going through those youthful, heady days, did not listen. As a result, the secret which he had carefully concealed from the whole world, had come out in the open.

As I have mentioned earlier as well, Nazir was a cold-hearted man. There were very few people who knew that he had a kind heart as well. Whatever his actions, he understood the good and bad behind them—which the average person does not. He did have a physical relationship with Sitara up till a point, but he did not want the same for Asif.

Asif was his nephew. One could say it was because of this relation that he did not approve of the union between Asif and Sitara. But I, who know all the crooked corners of Nazir's character, can say with confidence that even if it had been been any other man, he would still have warned him, 'Listen, stay away from that woman. I was the only one who was proud and strong, but I failed as well.'

Nazir was the epitome of morality, a morality that wears a harsh and rough garb. Upon Majeed's insistence, Nazir let go of both Asif and Sitara. Also because Asif had assured his uncle that their relation was pure.

Although Nazir left, he was not satisfied. Normally, he was a stubborn person, oblivious to mildness of any sort. But he could easily dive deep into the hearts of other people, and he knew Sitara in and out. He too had lived through the age that Asif was experiencing now. He had seen those highs which Asif might never see in his entire life. He was not satisfied at all.

After this incident, Sitara and Asif talked for a while. Promises of never leaving each other were made, among other such things. After that, like a true lover, Asif took her leave.

Sitara fixed her make-up, wore fresh clothes and called a taxi for P.N. Arora's place. Arora's health had, thanks to hakeems from Delhi, improved a little by now. His sunken cheeks had filled out a bit. Alnasir was also there. So was director Mehboob, and God knows who else.

Asif had definitely overcome a difficult stage in his life, but he had not stopped his visits to Sitara completely. And how could he? Sitara was like an ancient enchantress who had turned him into a fly and stuck him on a wall. There was only one escape—only a prince from one of those old fairy tales could, using his talisman, fight her sorcery and free Asif from her clutches.

I know, and I know it too well, that even the strongest of talismans would have no effect on Sitara. She is such a force that no one can tame her.

So the affair continued like this. Asif and Nazir's relationship was getting strained day by day.

Yes, I almost forgot to mention something. When Nazir had thrown Sitara out, Rafeeq Ghaznavi, the famous musican, had tried to patch things up. He had called Sitara, Nazir and Arora to his house. There were many rounds of liquor. Rafeeq, who is extremely eloquent, offered many pegs of liquor in his philosophical manner, but there was no resolution in sight. And when there was no resolution, there came to be a new situation. Sitara spent the whole night at Rafeeq's, who kept trying to convince her that there was no way out.

What is strange is that Rafeeq did not try to patch things up again, nor did Sitara go over to his place to hear that there was no way out. Maybe because Rafeeq did not appreciate one or two moves in Sitara's dance number. Or just maybe, Sitara felt that Rafeeq's singing was one or two notches off-key...nothing can be said with certainty.

Now, let us return to Sitara and Asif. Sitara had fallen head over heels for Asif, the young man who was completely inexperienced. She might have been the first woman in his life.

It is said that Nazir conducted another raid and caught them red-handed. I am not aware if anyone tried to mediate this time. Anyway, the matter was forgotten as Asif had again assured his uncle there was no such thing between him and Sitara. Whatever trouble that seemed to circle over Asif and Sitara's heads, seemed to have gone away for the time being. But the outcome of this was that one day, Asif disappeared.

The other day we heard that Sitara was also missing. After some inquiries it was found that she had gone on some pilgrimage. Had it been Hajj season, people would have definitely spread rumours that Hazrat Asif had gone for his Hajj.

I don't know where they went, but I got word

from Delhi that Sitara had accepted Islam, taken the Muslim name Allahrakhi and that she had married Asif, as per the Islamic tradition.

What his uncle Nazir must have gone through at this time, you can imagine. But what was interesting was that according to Hindu law, divorce was not possible. Once a woman is tied to a man, then even with a hundred excuses, she cannot separate from her husband. She can be an adultress, sit in the laps of hundreds of men, but she would still remain her husband's wife. Even if the Hindu man converts to another religion, there would be no difference in her original position. So, even though Sitara became Allahrakhi, K. Asif's begum, in the eyes of the law she was still Mrs Desai. The wife of that sick-looking Desai, who was struggling to eat two square meals a day.

Once this news was confirmed, I wrote to my heart's content in the columns of *Musavvir*. Nearly every week, the newly-wed couple was discussed in the most witty, interesting and humorous manner. When they returned to Bombay after their honeymoon, Nazir had to swallow a very bitter pill.

Once, I had the opportunity to go to the race

course. There, emerging from the crowd, I spotted Asif in a spotless shark-skin suit, with his hand around the sprightly Sitara's waist. As he got close, he first smiled and then started laughing, 'Wonderful, absolutely wonderful! The way you are spicing things up and writing in your columns is delightful.'

Sitara frowned and moved away to one side. But Asif did not pay her any attention and continued talking calmly with me for a long time. As I have mentioned earlier, Asif is a man with a big heart and despite being uneducated, has the capability of understanding a joke and laughing at it.

Now everyone in Bombay who had any interest in the film industry, knew that there was someone called Asif whom Sitara had married. The mussalmans of Punjab and UP would sit at the Irani hotels of Bhindi Bazaar and Mohammad Ali Road with cups of tea, and express their unbridled happiness that a Muslim brother had managed to convert an infidel and married her.

Many of them said that now Asif should not let her act in films.

Many said that though there was no harm in her acting, she should definitely observe purdah when stepping out of the house.

Many said, 'Forget it—it's all a cheap stunt.'

Well, as far as I know, Asif had legally married Sitara. But when I asked him after some time, 'Why hero, is Sitara actually your wedded wife?' he laughed, 'What nikah and what marriage?'

Now only God knows what the real matter was, and what the real matter is.

Asif did not have a house of his own. Both of them stayed at Khudadad Circle in Dadar and lived like free souls. Sitara had a car in which they roamed around town.

I have a feeling that Asif had convinced Lala Jagat Narayan in Delhi to give him money to make a film. He had probably taken some advance too, which is why he had money to splurge.

Asif had this great quality—his self-confidence. He did not have even an iota of inferiority complex. He would defeat big directors and story writers with his God-given gift. I called this gift of his a 'house sense', even in front of Asif. But he never seemed to mind.

When Asif turned director, he did not become conservative or jaded like the other directors, his horizons did not narrow. He invited intelligent minds to present good suggestions, which he accepted happily.

God only knows how I meander from one topic to another. But I would like to share a joke here which is interesting, as it is related to me.

During those days, Asif was making *Phool*.* One day, I was in my flat at Clare Road when I heard non-stop honking from downstairs. I stepped out into the balcony and saw a big car parked there. When I leaned against the railing, Asif stuck his big head out from the back seat and smiled. I said, 'Come, what is the matter?'

He opened the door and said something to Sitara, who was sitting next to him. Then he said to me, 'I'll come and tell you.'

Then that huge car's engine started up and, in the blink of an eye, it sped out of the Adelphi Chambers complex.

Asif turned towards the stairs.

I opened the door. Asif entered within a minute, shook my hands excitedly and said, 'I have come to read my story to you.'

**Phool* (1945) was K. Asif's directorial debut.

I joked, 'You should know that I charge a fee for this.'

Asif did not say a word and turned on his heel. I called out to him and even ran after him, but he did not listen. All he said was that he would return with the fee and then read his story to me, else he wouldn't.

I was very embarrassed that I had cracked such a joke with him—I was hoping that he would take it in the same spirit in which I had said it. But somehow, things turned topsy-turvy and he left.

When I went back up to my flat, I narrated the incident to my wife. She told me very clearly that I had acted stupidly. As he was not a close friend, I couldn't be so informal with him. This was true too—we were not that close. Both of us, by nature, spoke frankly, even to the extent of hurting others with our frankness. When I made the joke about the fee with him, I had absolutely no intentions of hurting him. Nor am I such a bania to demand payment beforehand. All I wanted was to hear the story, that was all.

I had heard many directors' third-class stories, not once but four–four times, because they were eager to hear my opinion. I had never asked for money for the time that I spent, for the time which was actually wasted.

I was sorry that I had upset Asif. I was thinking about him when there was a knock on the door. I opened it and saw a man standing there, who handed me an envelope. I was about to open it, when I heard the sound of a horn from downstairs. I went to the balcony and saw it was Sitara's car leaving the Adelphi Chambers gate.

I opened the envelope and found five notes of hundred each. There was a small note that came with it, 'The fees has been offered. I will return tomorrow.'

I was astounded.

At around nine the next morning, he arrived in the same car. Sitara was with him but she did not come upstairs. There was no need to knock, as the door was open and I was standing there to welcome him.

The moment he saw me he said, 'So doctor saheb... did you receive the fees?'

I was very embarrassed, trying to explain myself using the most appropriate words and returning those 500 rupees.

Asif laughed and sat down on the sofa, 'What are you thinking, Manto saheb? This is neither my money nor my father's. It is the producer's money. It was my mistake that I had come empty-handed. It was not my intention to get some work done for free. Of course, your time will be wasted, and you should be compensated for it. Now forget about this nonsense, and listen to the story.'

He did not give me another chance to say anything. He was sitting on the big sofa. I went and sat in the chair in front of it. I had never seen Asif narrating or even hearing a story. He rolled up the sleeves of his cotton shirt, undid the top button of his pants—which served as a belt—and crossed his legs on the sofa, ready to launch into the story.

'So, the title of the film is "Phool"... What do you think of the title?'

'It is nice, I suppose.'

'Thank you—now listen to the story. I will narrate it scene-by-scene.'

Then he started telling the story, which God knows who had written, in his special style. This style seemed to be that of a juggler. That is, not only did he modulate his voice according to the ups and downs of the plot, he would himself jump up and down with it. He would be on the sofa one minute, and the next his back would be up against the wall, then suddenly his head would be down and legs in the air—which would then land on the floor with a thump. Then immediately afterwards, he would squat back on the sofa. But then again, he would be standing up on the sofa, giving some speech as if he was campaigning for an election.

Finally, the story ended. It was a very long story. A few moments passed in a brief, diabolical silence. Then Asif asked, 'What do you think?'

Without thinking, I blurted out, 'It's ridiculous.'

Asif bit his lips furiously and embarrassed, sat down against the back of the sofa and asked in a strange voice, 'What did you say?'

Had it been anyone else, it's possible they would have floundered. But I am always very firm in such matters. So, unyielding, I repeated, 'I said that it is ridiculous.'

Asif tried hard to change my mind with his antics. But I do not like unnecessary bickering. He used to talk very loudly. So I thought the only solution would be to let loose my own vocal chords. I said to him, 'Listen, Asif saheb. Please get a heavy boulder, put it on my head. Get a bigger hammer and smash that boulder on my head. I would still stay that the story is ridiculous.'

I said all of this in a very loud voice. Getting down from the sofa back, he came forward. Taking my hand in his and kissing it he said, 'By God, it *is* ridiculous. This is exactly what I wanted to hear from you.'

I thought that maybe he was joking. But then I realized he was very serious. So then, we started thinking about changing and revising the story.

The funny story has ended. It is most definitely related to my personality. But the reason I told it here was to mark out the difference between the characters of Sitara and Asif.

Much time passed and Asif and Sitara continued to live as husband and wife. But here, I have to recall another funny anecdote.

This is about the time when Asif and I were not friends, and Sitara was not in his life. K. Asif had, I'm not exaggerating, thousands of pimples on his face—which are said to be signs of youth. I think if the signs of youth are so ugly and painful, God forbid that anyone is blessed with youth (I am thankful to God that I myself hadn't had these).

Every time I looked at his face, it seemed like a beehive and would cause me great anguish. I am half a hakeem too. As per my knowledge, and after consulting some of my doctor friends, I bought many medicines for him. But they were of no use. The pimples remained as they were. Though after Sitara came into his life, his face cleared up in a few months. Only the spots remained.

Listen to another funny anecdote. Kamal Amrohi and I were working together at Bombay Talkies. Discussions were going on to shape his story, 'Mahal', appropriately for a film. During that time, a small but painful pimple appeared on his right cheek. He mentioned the pain to me.

I said, 'There is a very simple solution, which is very effective too.'

'What is it?' he asked.

'Do you know where Sitara lives?' I said.

'Yes, of course. Why not?'

'Then do one thing. Make a trip to the staircase of her house and come back. But listen—do not go inside.'

Kamal was intelligent. He understood what I meant and laughed for a long time.

The anecdotes have ended.

Asif and Sitara lived a married life for a long time. Now, they stayed in a flat in Mahim—yes, that is where they stayed. I'm pretty sure it was Mahim, as I went there many times. There was a street across the church on Lady Jamshedji Road, at the end of which was a three-storeyed building, and I think Sitara's flat was on the third floor.

I got the opportunity to visit the place a number of times. During those days, after making *Phool*, I think Asif was trying to prepare for *Anarkali*. Kamal Amrohi had written the story. But he was probably not satisfied with it, as he had called many people to inject freshness into it. I was one of those many people.

I would reach there around eight in the morning. An old woman, who used to wear a fine muslin sari, would open the door. I would get irritated just looking at her. I felt as if a sorceress from *Alif Laila* had opened the door.

I would go inside and sit on the sofa. From the adjacent room, which I think was the bedroom, I could hear noises that shook my soul to the core. Asif would appear after a while, feeling his lips with his tongue, as was his habit. His dishevelled appearance was quite a sight—his cotton kurta was torn here and there, bruises on his neck and chest, messy hair, and quite out of breath. After the normal exchange of greetings, he would slump on the ground. A while later, Sitara would a send a bowl for Asif which had some sort of kheer, I don't know what. Slowly, unwillingly, Asif would finish the bowl. And then we would start our work, which was largely based on gossip.

Quite some time passed. Sitara and Asif seemed very close to each other. But I don't know what happened, as one day I heard that Asif was marrying a close relative of his. The date had been fixed and he was about to leave for Lahore with some of his close friends.

I was very busy those days. Else, I would have definitely met him and asked what the situation was. But I did not get the chance. Then one day, I bumped into him somewhere. When I asked him casually, he only said, 'I have decided to end that story, so that's it.'

He was in the car while I was on foot. He was in a rush too, so we couldn't talk much. After a few days I got to know that he had left with a big group of friends. Then the news came that his wedding in Lahore had taken place with great pomp and show. Endless barrels of liquor had been emptied, with courtesans performing in colourful mehfils for the guests. And then I heard that Asif had returned to Bombay with his brand-new wife, and had rented half a bungalow at Pali Hill in Bandra. Though, later we we found out that Nazir had the entire bungalow and given half of it to his nephew.

This was a very happy development. I did not know about Sitara's reaction to all this. But what I do know is that she would visit Arora quite often. And, he too would frequent her place.

Asif was staying at Pali Hill in those days, with his brand-new wife. I think he was busy preparing for *Mughal-e-Azam* at that time. The story of this film was written by Kamal Haider Amrohi. But Asif was not satisfied with it. He had taken suggestions from many writers, but he still remained dissatisfied.

I can tell you many stories on this subject. But that would not solve any purpose. What is worth mentioning though, is that Asif and his brand-new bride, who had gotten married with great pomp, stayed together for a while. Thereafter, it was seen that Asif saheb would be absent from his house, and spend his nights with Sitara.

The marriage did not last long. Nazir's young son also stayed there. I don't know what happened that made Asif stop going to his wife. There was unpleasantness. And then we got to know that a divorce was about to happen. All this time, Asif regularly visited Sitara.

From all this, one can figure out that Sitara was a skilful operator. Even a brand-new wife could not compete with her. So, after a few months, Asif's wife went back to her house and later, we found out that they had gotten divorced.

Now Asif and Sitara were together again. There were many rumours about Asif's previous wife making the rounds. But I do not wish to mention those as I am not sure about the truth behind those stories.

All I know is that Asif had married. There were elaborate get-togethers in Lahore. After that, Asif came to Bombay with his wife. He stayed at Pali Hill and left his wife within two–three months. What could have possibly been the reason, besides Sitara?

Sitara was a woman who had the ability to target men. She knew all the methods of seducing men. Or rather, one could say she knew how to make them completely useless for other women. This was the reason why Asif left his wife and went back to Sitara. She possessed that magnetism.

Asif had married within his family. There are many famous legends about that family. But I do not wish to talk about them. Asif had left his married wife. Maybe because she did not possess the qualities of Sitara. Or maybe because Asif was not interested in virgins. In any case, everyone knows the end result.

Asif's brand-new wife had left and he was living with Sitara again. Many bizarre rumours surfaced during this time, but I do not really wish to comment on those.

I have written this article. I am sure Asif will not be angry with me. That is because he is a gracious man. Sitara will get upset, for sure. But she will forgive me after a while. That is because she, too, does not have a small heart. She is a towering woman, although her height isn't much. I don't know what kind of a man she thinks me to be. But I consider her to be a woman who is born, maybe, once in a hundred years.

Translator's Acknowledgements

I did not realize when translation became such a passion for me. It could have happened while translating Gulzar saab's poetry for my PhD thesis, or perhaps after teaching the diploma course in translation at Jamia Millia Islamia, year after year. I can't put a finger on it. But now, I have reached a point where I wake up in the middle of the night, struggling for the right word.

When it comes to translation, there is never a right or wrong word, per se. There is a good word, and a better word. It all depends on how well acquainted the translator is with the cultural nuances of the source language, along with her command over the target language. There are always words, phrases and idioms steeped in a cultural milieu, which is almost impossible to replicate in the target language. In all such cases, I have made honest and desperate attempts to retain the cultural fabric of the original to the best of my ability.

Translating Manto was a bigger challenge because of his use of obscure colloquial language, and his sly, ironic wordplay. Manto never minced words and refused to sugarcoat the ugliness of society. His characters spoke in the language of their social milieu. The test was to be able to translate the nuances and connotations so wrapped up in that bygone era to which the author belonged.

There are many people who helped me with this book. To begin with, I would like to thank my friend Ruchi Singh, who believed that I could do this.

During my translation, I pestered Khalujaan (Mr Habibur Rahman Chighani) every time I got stuck with some word steeped in an obscure cultural context. This led to hours of deliberation over the phone. At one point, we even thought that we needed to develop a special dictionary for Manto. Thank you, Khalujaan, for being so patient with me.

Zarina khala (Ms Zarina Bhatty), thank you for helping me through the very interesting sketch of Sitara.

I would also like to thank Mr Jameel Gulrays, who introduced me to the humour in Manto's writings.

Thank you, Prof Shamim Hanfi for sorting out my last minute confusions and queries.

Thank you Anurag Basnet, Kartikeya Jain, Ravi Singh and the team at Speaking Tiger for all the support and discussions that we have had during this time. I couldn't have asked for a better editorial team.

A special thanks also to Jezreel Sarah Nathan for one of the most striking covers that I have come across.

Amir and Sana, thank you for being there with me at all times. Thank you Ammi and Abbu. And lastly, thank you God, for bringing these people into my life.

Saba Mahmood Bashir

October 2019